Thoroughbred Legacy

Th[...]

Scandal ha[...]
award-winning Q[...] [...]e to
return this hors[...] [...]e!

Available September 2008

#5 *Millions to Spare* by Barbara Dunlop
Identifying with your captor is one thing. Marrying him
is quite another! But when reporter Julia Nash is
caught snooping, she's faced with saying goodbye to her
freedom…or saying *I do* to Lord Harrison Rochester!

#6 *Courting Disaster* by Kathleen O'Reilly
Race-car driver Demetri Lucas lives hard and fast—and he likes
his women to match. Until he meets the one woman who can
tempt him to slow down and enjoy the ride.

#7 *Who's Cheatin' Who?* by Maggie Price
Champion jockey Melanie Preston has a firm no-men-with-
secrets policy. Especially when it comes to her family's horse
trainer, who has more secrets than anyone that sexy should.…

#8 *A Lady's Luck* by Ken Casper
After one glance, widower Brent Preston finds himself
feeling emotions he thought long since buried. But pursuing
his gracefully elusive English lady may mean heading
straight into the arms of danger!

Available December 2008
#9 *Darci's Pride* by Jenna Mills
#10 *Breaking Free* by Loreth Anne White
#11 *An Indecent Proposal* by Margot Early
#12 *The Secret Heiress* by Bethany Campbell

Available as e-books at www.eHarlequin.com
#1 *Flirting with Trouble* by Elizabeth Bevarly
#2 *Biding Her Time* by Wendy Warren
#3 *Picture of Perfection* by Kristin Gabriel
#4 *Something to Talk About* by Joanne Rock

Dear Reader,

Thoroughbred horses are a specific breed, and throughout their history they've existed for one reason only: to win races. And even though their most desirable qualities are those of any premier athlete—speed, agility and a perfectly proportioned body that can run like the wind without shattering—there are no guarantees. Thoroughbred horse racing is a sport in which all is serendipity and chance. Anything can happen, and what does is impossible to predict.

Much like love.

Champion jockey Melanie Preston hates secrets, so the last man she'd trust is Marcus Vasquez, the world-renowned Thoroughbred trainer who refuses to reveal anything about his personal life. But when the brewing scandal surrounding her family's livelihood forces Melanie to go to work for Marcus, she learns that love, like racing, is all about taking a gamble.

Happy reading!

Maggie Price

Thoroughbred Legacy

WHO'S CHEATIN' WHO?

Maggie Price

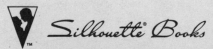

Silhouette Books

Published by Silhouette Books

America's Publisher of Contemporary Romance

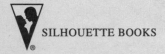 SILHOUETTE BOOKS

ISBN-13: 978-0-373-19924-2
ISBN-10:   0-373-19924-4

WHO'S CHEATIN' WHO?

Special thanks and acknowledgment are given to Maggie Price for her contribution to the Thoroughbred Legacy series.

Visit Silhouette Special Edition and Thoroughbred Legacy at www.eHarlequin.com.

Printed in U.S.A.

MAGGIE PRICE

Before embarking on a writing career, Maggie Price took a walk on the wild side and started associating with people who carry guns. Fortunately they were cops, and Maggie's career as a crime analyst with the Oklahoma City Police Department has given her the background needed to write true-to-life police procedural romances that have won numerous accolades, including a nomination for a coveted RITA® Award.

Maggie is a recipient of a Golden Heart Award, a Career Achievement Award from *Romantic Times BOOKreviews,* a National Readers' Choice Award and a Booksellers' Best Award, all for series romantic suspense. Readers are invited to contact Maggie at 416 N.W. 8th St., Oklahoma City, OK 73102-2604, or on the Web at www.MaggiePrice.com.

Special thanks to:

My husband, Bill Price,
who brought home a kazillion dinners so I didn't have
to cook while writing this book. (Then whisked me
off to the Orient for a much-needed respite!)

Linda Eubanks, for invaluable
and generous information. All liberties taken
in the name of fiction are my own.

Chapter One

Her shimmery gold gown glittering beneath the conservatory's bright lights, bridesmaid Melanie Preston excused her way through a crush of wedding guests. When she reached the towering French doors that led to the back veranda of the house, she flung one open and rushed out into the cool December night.

"Dammit," she muttered when she saw the man she'd followed there had already reached the far end of the long veranda, her grandfather's Irish wolfhound trotting along beside him.

With moonlight pouring down from the cloudless sky, she watched him descend the flagstone steps two at a time. Veering off, he strode toward the cobblestone walkway leading to the building that housed his office.

His *former* office, she amended. As of five o'clock

that afternoon, Marcus Vasquez was no longer head trainer at her family's Quest Stables, Kentucky's largest Thoroughbred racing facility.

With the world that had once seemed so perfect now in danger of collapsing like the legs of a newborn foal, Melanie couldn't blame him for terminating his employment after only a few months.

Because her gold Jimmy Choo ice-pick heels quashed all hope of catching up with Marcus on the cobblestone walkway, she paused in the center of the veranda. Rubbing her bare arms to ward off the December chill, she studied his retreating form.

He was tall, an inch or two over six feet with that fluid grace certain men were born with. He had coal-black hair, olive skin and deep-set dark eyes guarded by heavy brows. She was used to seeing him in work clothes, not a tuxedo, so when he'd shown up for her cousin's wedding, heat had spread through her in breath-stealing waves. It wasn't every man whose tux fit as though it had been tailored to a god's torso.

The man who hailed from a small town on Spain's Costa del Sol was handsome, distant and maddeningly aloof about all things personal.

Which he had every right to be. But Melanie had learned a devastating lesson about trusting any man so elusively reticent about himself and his past. So when Marcus hired on at Quest Stables and she felt the same damnable dark awareness stirring deep inside her that had once toppled her into emotional quicksand, it had scared her to death.

Five months later, that awareness still vibrated in her nerves whenever she got near him.

Hell, whenever she *thought* about him. Which was often. So she'd gone to great lengths to avoid him whenever possible.

Problem was, she was Quest's principal jockey and detouring around the head trainer hadn't exactly made for ideal working conditions. Instinct told her Marcus had let her get away with that solely because of the racing ban the Jockey Association had leveled against her parents' stables and every horse majority owned by the Prestons.

A shiver ran down her spine that had nothing to do with the crisp night air and everything to do with impending doom. Earlier that year, she'd ridden Leopold's Legacy to victory in the Kentucky Derby and Preakness. But hopes for a Triple Crown sweep had been dashed when a computer snafu at the Jockey Association required a resubmittal of the Thoroughbred's DNA. The resulting discovery that Leopold's Legacy had not been sired by the stallion of record, Apollo's Ice, sent shock waves through the racing world.

After that, things had gone from bad to worse. A cloud of suspicion now hung over the entire Preston family. Owners who'd boarded their horses at Quest for years had pulled them out and lodged them at other stables. And what had first been thought to be a data processing glitch took on a sinister edge when a horse also wrongly believed to have been sired by Apollo's Ice was poisoned to death in Dubai and a computer tech who had worked on the registry records at the Jockey Association disappeared shortly afterward. The chance for any Preston-owned stallions earning stud fees was gone, at least for the time being. And Leopold's Legacy's millions in winnings might have to be surrendered if it was proven he hadn't been sired by a Thoroughbred. A few longtime employees had been laid off due to the financial hit Quest had taken. Now, handsome, irritatingly aloof Marcus Vasquez, their head trainer, was leaving, too.

The first notes of a low, bluesy song drifted on the night air, prompting Melanie to glance over her shoulder. Despite the family's worsening problems, her mother was determined that life at Quest continue as normally as possible. So this December, as all others, the massive, two-story redbrick house shimmered with Christmas lights inside and out. Tonight, the lights were a fitting backdrop for Melanie's Australian cousin's wedding to Quest's female farrier.

Through the conservatory's big bay window, Melanie watched wedding guests chat while sipping champagne. Some headed for the area where furniture and potted plants had been removed to make a temporary dance floor. Others gathered before the huge Christmas tree decorated with silver ornaments that dominated one corner of the room.

The person who interested her most, however, wasn't inside the house.

The thought of going after Marcus had Melanie squaring her shoulders. She had planned to approach him right after her grandfather toasted the bride and groom. But the instant crystal flutes had clinked together, Marcus set his empty glass on the tray of a passing waiter, and headed out the French doors. Now, his long gait had taken him so far away she could barely make out his tall, moonlit form silhouetted against the security lights rimming the stables, the barn and various outbuildings.

By morning he would be gone.

She was surprised to find herself torn between a sense of relief and a tingle of regret.

In keeping with Marcus's maddening refusal to reveal anything about himself, no one at Quest seemed to know his plans for the future. But he was one of the country's top Thoroughbred trainers, so there were bound to be dozens of job opportunities available for someone with his formidable skills. Not just here in Kentucky, but nationwide. Worldwide.

Melanie flexed her fingers, then curled them into her palms. If she didn't talk to him, her conscience would niggle at her forever. She had no intention of offering an explanation for why she'd spent the majority of her time avoiding him. Or concede that she should have at least consulted him about her decision to work away from the main stables with the colt her younger brother felt sure would be the family's saving grace.

Tonight she simply intended to tell Marcus goodbye. Wish him luck. It was a matter of self-respect. She took her work as a jockey seriously. For reasons she couldn't explain, making sure that Marcus Vasquez understood that had become a priority.

And maybe, just maybe, knowing she'd gone to such lengths to detour around him scraped at her pride. It was too close to cowardice.

She wasn't a coward. Just a woman trying her best to stave off temptation in the form of a gorgeous Spanish hunk.

So, she would speak to Marcus as one professional to another. Keep the conversation businesslike, to the point and short. She just hoped she managed to hide the fact that he made her nervous. Edgy. Stirred up.

Melanie puffed out a breath that turned into a white cloud on the night air. With her pulse pounding and her nerves jittering, she wasn't sure how she was going to pull this off.

"Just get it over with," she muttered.

Hiking the skirt of her gown above her ankles, she headed down the veranda's stairs and went after him.

HIS GAZE FOCUSED out the window of what was now his former office, Marcus Vasquez watched Melanie Preston move along the cobblestone walk, the Irish wolfhound, Seamus, loping beside her as he'd done earlier at Marcus's side. The silver moonlight mixed with a pale glow from the small landscape lights dotting the gardens, making the woman and her massive escort seem almost ghostlike.

Since the path veered off in several directions, he wondered where the hell she was headed.

None of his business, he reminded himself. He'd had little say during his tenure at Quest over what the ace jockey did. As of this afternoon Marcus no longer worked for Thomas and Jenna Preston, so whatever had prompted their only daughter to leave her cousin's wedding reception and traipse around in the moonlight was none of his concern.

That didn't mean he couldn't enjoy the view. Leaning a thigh against the desk, Marcus tracked her progress along the walk.

Despite her ankle-wrecking heels and the walkway's uneven surface, Melanie's gait was fluid, like a dancer's. The only other time he'd seen her in a dress was at a gala last summer when he'd first arrived at Quest. Which was a good thing, because the way the gold material slithered against her slim hips was enough to revive a dead man.

He was very much alive.

Watching her, Marcus felt the hunger that he'd kept hidden since the moment they'd met stir inside him.

She was barely five feet tall, lean and agile. For the rest of his life, he would carry a mental picture of her from the video he'd watched uncountable times: Melanie Preston on Derby Day wearing Quest's bright racing silks, urging Leopold's Legacy to leap from the starting gate and hurtle onto the track. Barely fastened to the saddle, her entire body had lifted into the air like a butterfly preparing to take flight. Only her hands on the reins and the tips of both boots wedged in the stirrups still tied her to earth.

Marcus had worked his way up in the racing business on four continents. Without a doubt, she was the best jockey he'd encountered. If the scandal hadn't broken after the Preakness win, she most likely would have raced the stallion in the Belmont to a Triple Crown sweep.

She was also the most annoying jockey he had ever run across.

It wasn't simply that she'd made herself scarce

around the main stables since his first day on the job, choosing to work instead with her younger brother Robbie, who'd taken a colt named Something To Talk About to train on his own. The few times Melanie *had* shown up here in his office, her talk of implementing unproven approaches to stable management techniques had tried Marcus's patience.

It hadn't helped that during every exchange he'd been as aware of her striking blue eyes, sun-streaked blond hair and compact curves as he'd been of her words. He'd damn well had his share of X-rated fantasies about his boss's daughter.

Fantasies he hadn't allowed himself to act on. Not only because he had a policy never to mix business with pleasure. There was the small complication of his blood ties to the man who, Marcus had only recently learned, owned Apollo's Ice. Although there was no proof Nolan Hunter was involved in the scandal that had tarnished the Preston family's standing in the racing world and caused a fiscal disaster for their stables, Marcus doubted the Prestons would have hired him away from the Australian side of their family if anyone had known he was Hunter's half brother. And because of a promise made long ago, Marcus didn't intend to tell anyone.

Withholding that information from the Prestons weighed heavy on his shoulders, and Marcus had felt a measure of relief when he saw proof that their youngest son, Robbie, had developed the capabilities to step into the head trainer position. Confident that the horses and stables would be in good hands—and knowing it would ease the strain on the Prestons not to have to pay his hefty salary—had made it easy for Marcus to give notice that he would be moving on.

Even if he still had no idea where he would be moving on to.

He'd worked on farms and around tracks since he was ten. Stable boy, exercise boy, groom. Working his way up, hustling his way through. For the first time, he felt the dull ache of regret about leaving a certain place behind.

A certain woman. He almost felt cheated.

Grinding out an oath between his teeth, he pulled his gaze from the window. Turning away, he forced himself to dismiss thoughts of Melanie Preston. Tried to, anyway.

He worked in silence for a few minutes, loading a box with the personal items he carried to each job.

The instant she stepped through the office's open door, he scented her. The fragrance of warm skin mixed with the soft aroma of Chanel stirred the hunger he'd fought to keep leashed every damn time she got near him.

Repressing the storm of need brewing inside him, Marcus looked up from the box. "Shouldn't the sole bridesmaid be helping the bride and groom celebrate?"

"I imagine Shane and Audrey can do without me for a little while."

Melanie forced her mouth to curve while the deep timbre of Marcus's voice registered up and down her spine. Holy hell, why was it all she had to do was look at him and her knees went weak and her heart tumbled in her chest?

"What about you?" she asked. "Instead of packing,

shouldn't you be at the reception, catching up with all the Australian Prestons?"

"I spent most of the day wrapping up last-minute details. Packing the remainder of my things was at the bottom of my list, and I wanted to get it done tonight." He shrugged. "I plan on heading back to the reception when I'm finished here."

Great, Melanie thought. She could have just stayed at the house instead of chasing after him. "Well, I didn't want to let you get away without saying goodbye."

His killer dark eyes narrowed speculatively on her face. "For the most part, you've avoided me the entire time I've worked here. Now that I'm leaving, you feel the need to converse. Why?"

Oh, boy. "I didn't *avoid* you," she said. "Not exactly," she added when one of his dark brows crept up. "Robbie's convinced Something To Talk About will be our next champion. When Robbie took the colt off on his own to train, he asked me to work with him, too. My brother had a lot to prove to himself and the entire family. I wanted to help."

Because she could feel her nerves jumping, Melanie wandered along one wall of the office, pretending interest in the series of framed newspaper clippings of the stable's numerous Thoroughbred winners. Then there were the studio photographs of Quest's winning-est jockeys. Hers included.

She slid Marcus a sideways look. "I hope there are no hard feelings."

"Wouldn't be much point in them. You and Robbie proved two months ago that you know what you're doing when you took Something To Talk About to Dubai. Winning the Sandstone Derby is impressive."

"I'm just glad the Sandstone took place before Quest got hit with the international racing ban." Melanie paused before the credenza on which several trophies sat. Some were from races in which she had ridden the winners herself, and she couldn't help but wonder if she'd ever again get to race wearing her family's silks.

"Robbie will make a good head trainer for Quest," Marcus said.

With a huge ball of emotion wedged in her throat, Melanie turned from the credenza while Marcus placed a coffee mug inside the open box on the desk. "He will," she agreed. "You did a good job, too."

"I'd have done better if the ban hadn't stopped me from racing Quest's horses."

"So, where do you go from here?"

"To another job."

She waited expectantly for him to elaborate, but he continued scooping items out of a desk drawer, offering nothing more.

His silence reminded her of the reason the attraction she felt toward him made her want to run for the hills. Being duped by a lover who'd failed to mention he had a pregnant wife at home had taught Melanie the danger of trusting a man who didn't know what it meant to be forthcoming.

A man like Marcus Vasquez.

Which circled her back to the reason she'd sought him out tonight. To say goodbye.

"I should get back to the reception." She took the few

steps toward the desk and offered her hand. "I wish you the best, Marcus."

His gaze met hers. For a long moment, he said nothing. Did nothing.

Her lips parted slightly when she saw the change in his eyes, the deepening, the darkening as an emotion she was at a loss to identify grew. All she knew was that in the space of a heartbeat, something between them had changed.

He took her hand, his fingers sliding to link with hers. "Since you made a special trip down here in those ankle-wrecking heels to tell me goodbye, maybe we should make the most of it."

Her fingers clenched his reflexively. "Make the most of it?" His firm, calloused touch lodged a sudden pressure in her chest that made her breathing go shallow. The muscles in her stomach began to twist, tighten. Ache.

He smelled of soap, a fragrance that was clean and sharp. She fought the sudden urge to lean in, fill her lungs with his compelling scent.

"In Spain, it's believed that when two people part for what may be a very long time, they must share a kiss to seal their friendship."

"And if they don't?" she managed.

"It's their fate to become the deadliest of enemies."

A dangerous excitement heated her blood, sending a delicious sizzle of anticipation through her veins. Lifting her chin, she shook back her hair. "Well, we don't want that. Odds are good we'll cross paths again at various racetracks. It would be more comfortable for both of us if we were friends."

"Agreed."

She held her breath, waiting, watching, as his mouth drew closer, closer…. He was the last man she should allow to cross the barrier and touch her. Even as she told herself that, she voiced no protest, made no move to evade the kiss. She didn't want to evade it. Marcus Vasquez had played havoc with her libido for months, and she wanted to know how he kissed, how he tasted.

He'd be gone by morning. What harm could one kiss do?

She shivered at the first brush of his lips, blinking as if the contact had given her a shock. He held her gaze, his eyes dark and intense, mesmerizing. Then he settled his mouth over hers, and thought ceased. Her eyes drifted shut. Her hands slid beneath the jacket of his tux, her palms settling against his rock-hard chest.

He slanted his head, his lips parted, and he deepened the kiss until his tongue was in her mouth. The bottom dropped out of her stomach, her legs wobbled and her entire body tensed.

With one arm locked around her waist, Marcus slid his fingers into her hair. She tasted sweet, and she felt like heaven against him. He groaned deep in his chest and pressed closer. The scent of warm skin mixed with Chanel filled his head. He knew what it was like to be cheated out of something he wanted badly. Tonight, he'd be damned if he held himself back from taking what he'd wanted for so long.

While his mouth fed on hers, he spread his legs and inched closer, heat diffusing through him as his thighs brushed the outside of hers and his groin nudged her belly.

She was tiny and soft and feminine, and he wanted her.

When their kiss turned frenzied, arousal pounded through him. He wanted to tear his slacks open, rip apart the soft, thin material of her gown and take her right here on the desk. He wanted to watch her face when he filled her.

This need, this want of her was instantaneous and stronger than anything he'd known.

And all-around crazy, considering who he was currently ravishing.

That thought had desire dying like a flame suddenly doused.

What the hell was he doing? He no longer worked for Thomas and Jenna Preston, but he respected them. Marcus knew full well neither would thank him for doing his best to seduce their daughter before he left Quest.

Even if she had somehow unlocked emotions inside him that went far past attraction and challenge to verge on pain.

Melanie opened her eyes as Marcus stepped away. She felt dizzy, weak, as shaken as she had the first time she'd been bucked off a horse. Like a woman in a daze, she lifted a hand and touched her fingers to her lips, lips that felt hot and swollen and thoroughly kissed.

"I guess after that, we'll be friends for life," she managed.

He smiled, just the faintest curve of his lips. "At least."

"I should get back," she added, her body not receiving any of her brain's commands to move.

Marcus didn't move, either. He stood facing her, his eyes dark and unreadable. "I'll walk you there," he said after a long moment.

Her heart hammered in her head, echoing in her ears

like a train picking up speed in a tunnel. How was it possible to be stunned so thoroughly by the heat? To be swept away so quickly, to want so desperately what you knew you shouldn't have?

Where once the pull she felt toward him had scared her, the intensity of it now terrified her.

"You don't need to walk me." She swept an unsteady hand toward the box on the desk. "You're not done packing."

"I just finished." He added a file folder to the box, closed its flaps, then hefted it up with one arm. "I'll stow this in my car on the way back to the reception." Marcus glanced at the clock on the wall. "By now your cousin Tyler should be through performing his duties as his brother's best man. I want to catch up with him. Find out what's gone on at Lochlain Racing after I left Australia to work here."

"Fine." Hoping to heck her trembling legs continued to support her, Melanie turned and headed for the door. As she moved, she ran her tongue over her lips. Marcus's taste churned through her blood all over again.

What if she never managed to fully rid her system of his taste?

Thank goodness, she thought as he switched off the light and closed the door to the office. Thank goodness he'd be gone by morning.

Chapter Two

"I have a good feeling about the Outback Classic, Marcus." Pride, along with a deep Australian accent, shimmered in Tyler Preston's voice. "You should see Lightning Chaser now. These days, he eats up the ground."

With his mind only partly on the conversation, Marcus skimmed his gaze for what seemed the hundredth time around the conservatory brimming with music, flowers and elegantly gowned and tuxedoed guests.

Audrey Griffin Preston looked stunning in snowy white lace glimmering with pearls, her face luminous as she danced with her tall, sandy-haired husband, Shane. The newlyweds shared the dance floor with numerous family members and guests, including the groom's parents and grandparents, who'd flown in from Australia for the wedding festivities.

A knot of people had gathered near the towering Christmas tree brimming with silver ornaments and white lights that looked like tiny stars trapped in its limbs. Other guests mingled around the room.

Since he had walked Melanie back to the reception, Marcus knew she was somewhere in the crowd. At the moment, though, he couldn't locate her.

Which shouldn't matter at all.

But it did.

Dammit, he might have been responsible for initiating that kiss, but he didn't thank her for unlocking needs he had no intention of satisfying. He'd grown up watching the devastating toll love had taken on his mother, and that was enough for him to never want to go anywhere near that same path. Ever.

More and more, leaving Quest looked like a smart move. He just wished he'd get over the dragging regret that had plagued him since he gave Andrew Preston his notice. Regret that now seemed to have settled like a stone in his gut with the knowledge he'd likely never again have another taste of the woman he'd held in his arms less than an hour ago.

Dammit, why did that seem to matter so much?

"Earth to Vasquez."

The comment had Marcus shifting his attention back to Tyler. The general manager of Lochlain Racing was tall and lanky, with dark hair and a tanned face made ruddy by hours spent under the Australian sun. At the moment, his green eyes were narrowed speculatively on Marcus.

"The way you're taking the crowd apart makes me think you're on the lookout for someone." Sliding one flap of his tuxedo jacket back, Tyler slipped a hand into the pocket of his slacks while studying the crowd. "A woman, maybe?"

"I'm just checking out who came to witness your brother tie the knot," Marcus said, avoiding a direct answer.

He sipped the scotch he'd opted for over the champagne that flowed freely. To ensure the subject veered away from the reason he'd taken up residence in a spot with a prime view of all the celebrants, he turned the conversation back to a subject close to Tyler's heart. "As for Lightning Chaser, does he still like to make the other horses try to catch him?"

"Every time he gets on a racetrack," Tyler answered with a wide smile. "I have high hopes for him in the upcoming Classic."

Marcus thought about a black cloud that could mar the race. "What about Sam Whittleson?" he asked, referring to the man whose horse had beat Lightning Chaser in an Australian race several months back. After it was discovered Whittleson's horse had been pumped full of steroids, Lightning Chaser was declared the winner. Bad blood ensued when Whittleson claimed his horse had been sabotaged. There were those who speculated Tyler could be responsible. "He might be interested in payback."

"If Whittleson tries anything, he'll be sorry." The hard snap in Tyler's voice left no doubt that his threat was anything but idle.

The music swept up into a crescendo then ended, followed by a round of applause for the bride and groom. Tyler set his drink aside. "It's time for me to claim a dance with my new sister-in-law."

Moments after Tyler smiled goodbye and headed for the dance floor, Marcus spotted Melanie. She was on the far side of the conservatory, leaning down to say something to her nieces, the twin daughters of her brother Brent, Quest's head breeder. Both girls had their brown hair in braids and wore knee-length dresses made out of the same gold material as Melanie's. Smiling, she whispered something to them, and the twins giggled.

All so innocent, Marcus thought. Far from innocent was the hunger emanating from him as he studied their aunt's soft, angular profile. The attraction had been there from the moment he met Melanie on his first day at Quest, sitting in the stables with her boots off. But now he'd had a taste of her. No mere attraction had ever made him ache the way she was making him ache. And no sexual desire had ever made him feel as if he were inexorably sinking into hot lava.

When he caught himself imagining what it would be like to have another taste of her, he knew he was in trouble. Draining his scotch, he decided to say goodbye to the Prestons and head to his quarters for one last night at Quest. He had no idea where he would be twenty-four hours from now.

"Marcus, have you got a minute?"

He turned to find Demetri Lucas standing inches away. Earlier, Marcus had overheard someone mention that the recently retired race car driver, who was engaged to Elizabeth Innis, a Preston cousin, had missed the wedding due to business concerns. Since Demetri was dressed in a casual sweater and slacks, Marcus theorized he had just arrived.

"I have more than a minute," Marcus said, shaking the hand Demetri offered. A native of Greece, he had a dusky Mediterranean complexion, black hair and dark eyes. It was well-known Demetri was a close friend of Hugh Preston, the family patriarch who'd built Quest from the ground up. Taking advantage of Hugh's legendary ability to sense when a horse had the makings of a champion, Demetri had followed his mentor's recommendations when buying a dozen Thoroughbreds over the years. Currently those horses were stabled at Quest, but unaffected by the North American and international racing ban on horses majority owned by the stables.

"Is Elizabeth here?" Marcus asked.

"Unfortunately, no. Her concert tour's in London right now. She called earlier with news that the rest of her European tour is sold out."

"Impressive," Marcus said. And because he and Demetri had spent time working with the horses Demetri kept stabled at Quest, he asked, "Do you have questions about your horses?"

"Always, but they can wait. Right now, I want to talk about you."

"Me?"

"I know today was your last working day at Quest. Do you have another job lined up?"

"Not yet. I plan to start looking in earnest after the holidays."

"This may be my lucky day." Demetri beamed the

smile that had shown up on the covers of international racing magazines, as well as *People* and *GQ*. "Yours, too."

"How so?"

"Have you ever wanted to own part of a Kentucky horse-racing stable?"

Marcus raised a brow. "The thought has crossed my mind." Then had been quickly rejected, and not just because of the heart-stopping amount of money that would be involved. Owning a stable meant putting down roots, something he had never had a desire to do. Keeping loose, free and unfettered had always been more to his liking.

He thought again about the heavy regret that had hounded him over the past month. The idea of moving to another job simply didn't carry the same feeling of rightness it always had in the past.

He made a quick survey of the wedding guests, sought out Melanie. She was dancing with the groom now. Shane was her cousin, yet seeing her in the arms of another man made Marcus's jaw go tight. Lord, he had it bad.

"Hugh knows about this deal and he's given me the use of his study upstairs," Demetri said, pulling Marcus's attention back. "If you're interested, you and I can talk business there in private."

"I won't know if I'm interested until I hear what you have to say. But I'm curious."

Minutes later, Marcus and Demetri stepped into the study, a warm, vibrant room with thick rugs and polished brasses. Dark walnut paneled one wall; floor-to-ceiling bookshelves lined the other three. The windows were tall and narrow, diamonds of leaded glass that looked out on the dark December night.

"As of today, Elizabeth and I own Rimmer Stables," Demetri said, handing Marcus a crystal tumbler of scotch. He settled into the red leather chair beside Marcus's, both grouped in front of the enormous gray stone fireplace. "Rimmer's one hour from here. Are you familiar with it?"

"Not with the stables, but their horses. They've had some champions in the past." Pulling details from his memory, Marcus stared into the flames dancing in the fireplace. "The distant past," he clarified. "I understand the original owner, Jack Rimmer, died a couple of years ago. Apparently his son doesn't have the experience or know-how to keep the stables a success."

"Which is why Rimmer's widow put the place on the market. I've got the same problem she does. Elizabeth and I own the stables now, but neither of us have the expertise or the time to operate them. That's where you come in. We need a partner, Marcus. One who knows horses inside and out, and has what it takes to run a successful business. I'm not talking just about horses but the facility itself. Rimmer junior has kept up with the maintenance on the stables and other structures, but not on the main house. Seeing to that is high on my list."

"And not cheap."

Demetri grinned. "Luckily, winning Formula Gold races has made my financial standing very comfortable. Not to mention the purses my Thoroughbreds have brought in. And Elizabeth's latest album debuted at number one on the charts. Money isn't an issue."

"That will definitely ease the way." Marcus angled his chin. "Speaking of your Thoroughbreds, I take it you'll be moving them from Quest to Rimmer?"

"Which I plan to rename Lucas Racing," Demetri said. "And, yes, I'll have my horses transported there." Demetri sipped his scotch. "You're probably thinking that pulling my Thoroughbreds from Quest when it's in financial trouble is a slap in the face to Hugh and all the other Prestons. And not a particularly wise move, considering that I'm engaged to a Preston cousin."

"I don't have a clue how family politics work, so I'll leave that up to you," Marcus said.

Thanks to a father who'd rejected his pregnant mistress and their son, Marcus had no idea whether Demetri was stubbing his toe when it came to dealing with future relatives. But Marcus did know the Thoroughbred racing business.

"You've held back moving your horses longer than other owners. Some took their stock out the day after the U.S. ban went into effect. I imagine the Prestons appreciate the loyalty you've shown. And starting up your own stable more than justifies the move."

"After I get my horses relocated to Lucas Racing, I plan to purchase more. The Prestons own a number of Thoroughbreds. If selling some to me will help their cash flow problems, everybody gains." Demetri sipped his scotch. "You know every horse stabled here. I'd like you to think about which ones would be a good addition to my new venture."

"All right," Marcus said. It wouldn't take any thought

on his part, though, to choose the number one horse on the list. Robbie Preston had first clued Marcus in on the fact that Something To Talk About was special. Robbie had been right. The colt Melanie had raced to a magnificent win in Dubai's Sandstone Derby before the international ban took effect was in the star-making class. He wouldn't just break records, he would smash them to bits. But only if he could race.

Marcus frowned when he thought about the special affinity Melanie had for the colt. He was aware that she visited its stall every evening. Several times, he'd stood unobserved in a shadowy corner, listening to her coo to the gray horse with white stockings while treating him to a slice of pear.

It was clear she loved the colt. Marcus didn't have to wonder what her reaction would be if her family agreed to sell the horse.

"I've got some terms in mind for our proposed partnership," Demetri said. "Most are negotiable."

"I'm listening." Sipping his scotch, Marcus settled back in his leather chair.

"What do you say?" Demetri asked, after outlining the terms. "Are you interested?"

"So far," Marcus said. The offer sounded almost too good to be true, and he wanted time to think about it. Look at it from all angles. "One thing, if I sign on, I want total authority over the stable staff. If I decide to hire someone, or an employee needs firing, I don't want to have to come to you for permission before I can act."

"Agreed."

"I'll go tomorrow and take a look at your new

stables." Marcus rose, offered Demetri his hand. "I'll get back to you soon with an answer."

SHE MISSED MARCUS.

Melanie frowned at the knowledge while she groomed Something To Talk About. They'd had a good exercise this sunny December morning, flying out across the fields, streaking over the rises through the cold whip of wind while the air roared with the thunder of hooves.

During the whole of it, Marcus Vasquez had clung to her thoughts like a troublesome burr.

It had been nearly a week since she'd last seen him at Shane and Audrey's wedding reception. Almost that long since she'd heard Marcus had gone into partnership with Demetri Lucas and her cousin.

"Demetri is engaged to my cousin, Elizabeth," Melanie informed the colt as she ran her hands up his legs to feel for heat in strained tendons. "You met her— the country-and-western singer I introduced you to a month or so ago? She thought you were the most handsome thing on four legs she'd ever seen."

As though he understood, Something To Talk About nickered.

Melanie glanced up. "You're right, Elizabeth's gorgeous. And, man, can she sing—she's got a boatload of Grammy awards to prove it, too. Anyway, she's in Europe right now on a concert tour. Which means she's not around to give me the inside scoop about what's going on at the new stables."

Specifically, what was going on with Marcus Vasquez, Melanie added mentally.

Frustrated over her seeming inability to get her mind off the man for more than five minutes, she lifted the colt's foreleg to check the hoof.

It was maddening to find herself thinking about Marcus so often. He was gone from Quest—she had *wanted* him gone because he was nothing but total, sexy-as-hell temptation. Even so, she missed him.

It was that damn kiss. She couldn't stop her mind from doing slo-mo replays of it. And with each replay her nipples popped to attention and the spot deep between her thighs went all tight and achy.

Which was the last thing she needed. Wanted.

She'd learned her lesson about trusting a man who had a lot in common with an iceberg: far more lurking underneath than showed on the surface. With every intuitive fiber of her being, she knew that Marcus was the iceberg king.

She should have never let him kiss her. Never let herself kiss him back.

"Why am I even thinking about that man when I have a big guy like you right here?" she asked, nuzzling the colt's neck.

Something To Talk About blew out a soft breath. Pure pleasure.

Smiling, Melanie met his big brown eyes. "I love you, too," she murmured while retrieving one of the brushes from her grooming kit. "When the ban's lifted and we can race again, you and I are going to kick some serious butt. Show everyone you've got what it takes to be a champ. You'll have cute mares falling all over you after that."

The horse snorted and flicked his ears.

Melanie heard the dull thud of boots coming along the concrete floor. She looked across her shoulder in time to see Joe Newcomb, one of Quest's longtime grooms, step up to the stall door. He was a burly man, running to fat, growing bald.

Looks were deceiving. Melanie's grandfather had told her that, in his day, Joe had been the toughest man ever to put his foot in a racing stirrup. "Morning, Joe."

"Morning. Your brothers asked me to tell you they need to talk to you."

"Which brothers?"

"Andrew and Robbie. They're waiting in the office off the tack room." Joe dipped his head toward the colt. "You want me to, I'll finish up grooming him."

"Thanks, Joe." Melanie handed him the brush and headed out of the stall.

She hoped whatever it was her brothers wanted to talk to her about would get her mind off Marcus.

"YOU'VE DONE WHAT?" Melanie asked minutes later. She stood at the edge of the desk in the small, cluttered general-use office, her heart in her throat.

"I've sold an interest in Something To Talk About," Andrew Preston said again from the chair behind the desk. With one hand, he stroked Seamus's head while the Irish wolfhound gazed up at him adoringly, tongue lolling out of one side of his mouth, tail wagging hard enough to achieve liftoff.

Melanie had always thought her oldest brother was one of the most handsome men she'd ever seen. She still did. But he was Quest's business manager, and over the past months, stress from the scandal had etched deep lines at the corners of his eyes and mouth.

She knew Quest's financial status was bleak. Understood the logic behind the sale. That didn't stop her heart from breaking at the thought of losing the colt she loved so fiercely.

"Something To Talk About can't race, not as long as we own a majority interest in him." The comment came from her younger brother, Robbie. Tall and lean, he stood with one shoulder propped against a wall, his arms folded over his chest. His dark blue eyes held the same grimness as Andrew's.

"If he isn't allowed to start proving himself in upcoming races, it'll waste his entire two-year-old year," Robbie continued. "You know that as well as I do, Mel. You and I spent the past months training him to get him on a racetrack, not keep him off."

"I know." She understood that Robbie, as the new head trainer, had to shift his focus to the overall needs of Quest rather than the single colt he'd trained. Still, it seemed her chest would explode from the sheer force of the emotion churning there. "Who bought the majority interest in Something To Talk About?"

"Lucas Racing," Andrew replied. "That's the name of the company Demetri, Elizabeth and Marcus have formed. And the name they've given the facility they bought recently. The place used to be Rimmer Stables."

"Marcus is an excellent trainer, Mel," Robbie added. "He'll do right by the colt."

She nodded slowly. Of course, Marcus would have recognized the colt's potential. Buying an interest in

Something To Talk About was a wise move to get the new company off the ground.

"When do they plan to pick him up?" she asked, her voice barely a whisper.

"This afternoon."

"YOU'RE GOING TO DO just fine at your new home," Melanie told the colt. She'd waited to come back to Something To Talk About's stall until her emotions had settled. Horses were smart, they could sense when someone was upset. She didn't want to disturb the colt's emotional balance.

You shouldn't be upset, Melanie lectured herself. Over her lifetime, she'd felt a fondness for dozens of horses that had been stabled at Quest, then moved on for one reason or another. That was the nature of the horse-racing business, and she accepted it.

Just as she should be able to accept losing Something To Talk About to another stable.

With trembling hands, she used a knife to slice a pear in half. "You already know Marcus." She held out one of the halves, which the colt nipped from her open palm. "Even though he didn't train you from the beginning like Robbie did, Marcus'll take good care of you. Make you into a champion. And won't it be a kick in the pants if someday I wind up riding another horse in the same race with you?"

She laid the knife aside, then pressed her cheek to the colt's. "God, I'm going to miss you."

Her shoulders instinctively stiffened at the same instant the horse shifted.

"I expect he'll miss you, too," Marcus said.

It didn't surprise her that she hadn't heard him approach the stall. Nor did it surprise her that despite not hearing him, she'd sensed he was there. The air around her changed, she thought, whenever Marcus was nearby.

She took a steadying breath and forced herself to turn.

He stood in the stall's open door, looking all tough and rangy and fit in a sweater as black as his eyes, and faded jeans with bleach stains splattered over one thigh. Just seeing him again had something in her leaping to attention.

What is it about this man? I take one look at his face, inhale a whiff of his scent, and I'm aching to tear off his clothes. And mine, as well.

Not good, she thought. After all, he hadn't come to Quest to see her. He'd come to conduct business. So, she would accommodate him.

"You know horses, understand them, that's a given," she said. "But does Demetri?"

Marcus studied her a long moment. "A lot of owners don't *know* horses. What are you getting at?"

"Demetri races cars. Or he did before he retired. I hope he understands that horses aren't like race cars. You can't just park them in a new place and expect them not to notice. Not to get upset."

"I'll be sure and tell him," Marcus said, his eyes lingering on her.

She wore her blond hair anchored back with clips. Her jeans were snug and faded to a soft blue-gray that matched her down vest. Under that she wore a sweater the color of pale, creamy caramel. Her boots appeared old, scuffed and serviceable. Despite her work clothes, she wore earrings with bright stones that glittered beneath the stable's lights.

Seeing the sparkle of the stones had Marcus wondering if she'd also taken time that morning to dab on Chanel. Nearly a week had passed since they'd kissed, and the memory of her scent still kept him awake at night. He wasn't sure he would ever get it out of his system.

Wasn't sure he wanted to.

Which told him right there he should stay away from her. He'd grown up watching just how miserable love could make a person, and he wanted no part of it. He could have easily sent one of his grooms with a trailer to transport the colt. Instead, he'd come himself. Solely because he wanted to see *her*. And find out for himself if she was as upset about losing the horse as he suspected she'd be.

And maybe, just maybe, toss out the offer he'd been considering. The offer he kept telling himself was all sorts of crazy.

"Will you race him soon?" she asked, while holding out her palm to offer the horse a slice of pear.

"If I decide he's ready." While Something To Talk About munched on the pear, Marcus gave him an appraising look. The colt was strongly built and had already demonstrated in Dubai that he had the hunger and ability to win. "Florida's Gulf Classic race is on New Year's Day."

"That's less than a month away."

"True."

"You know full well that changing facilities and

trainers and jockeys all at the same time could affect Something To Talk About's desire to win."

Marcus lifted a brow. "Did he tell you that when you were talking to him?"

"He tells me lots of things," Melanie countered, her chin inching up. "One being that you need to give him time to get used to his new home and new people before you expect him to race."

"He'll settle in just fine at Lucas Racing. I've got a nice stall lined with fresh hay waiting for him."

Marcus watched Melanie's blue eyes narrow when he stepped through the open door. "As for trainers, Something To Talk About already knows me."

He moved farther into the stall. When he paused beside Melanie, he caught the faintest echo of her scent. Instantly, heat coiled in his gut.

Marcus set his jaw. He could feel himself falling into something with her that he couldn't handle, didn't want. But hell if he could stop thinking about her. Or stay away from her.

The offer he'd been considering might be crazy, but he didn't care. Not when he still had her taste in his system. And wanted more.

He ran his palms over the colt's head and throat, skimming, stroking, checking. "He won't have to get used to a new jockey if you come to work for me."

He had the satisfaction of seeing sheer astonishment in Melanie's face. "What did you say?"

"You heard me."

She shook her head. "That's impossible. I can't leave Quest."

"If times were normal, I wouldn't expect you to. But the instant questions arose about the lineage of Leopold's Legacy, things started going downhill. I worked here, Melanie. I *know* how bad things are."

The instant before she tore her gaze from his, he caught the gleam of tears in her eyes. He had to hold himself back from reaching for her.

"You're a damn fine jockey. But right now with the ban in place, you can't race any horses majority owned by Quest. Come to work for me, and I'll have you back on a racetrack as soon as possible."

"I can't walk out on my family." When she looked back at him, he saw she had fought back the tears. But he could hear the emotion in her voice.

"Walking out isn't what you'll be doing," Marcus countered. He moved around the horse, running his hands down its flank. "Think about it this way. Your family still owns forty-nine percent of this guy. Any races you ride him in and win money, they get a portion of the purse. Seems to me that's an important way for you to help your family."

Marcus met her gaze over the horse's broad back. He could see she was wavering, but still wasn't convinced. "You said it yourself, Something To Talk About will do better if he's around people he knows. You sign on at Lucas, he'll have me and you. Otherwise, you'll still be *here,* and he'll be *there.* That happens, there'll be some other jockey riding him. I doubt that's going to sit well with you."

Watching Melanie, Marcus saw clearly how loyalty to her family tugged at her. Family loyalty was something he knew little about. Instead, he knew how it felt to be cheated out of something because of blood kin. He was illegitimate, and his own father had refused to acknowledge he even existed. The almost-obsessive love his mother felt for her married lover had stolen any hope she might create a happy, fulfilling life with another man.

"Don't talk yourself out of this opportunity, Melanie. Your grandfather, your parents, your brothers— none of them would thank you for turning it down on their account."

She remained silent while skimming her hand along the colt's jaw. After a moment she said, "I need time to think this over."

"Understandable. Just to let you know, housing is a part of the package."

"Housing?"

"It's an hour's drive from here to Lucas. I doubt you'd want to commute every day." He lifted a shoulder. "For now, you'll have a staff apartment. There's a lot of remodeling going on in the main house, but once it's done you may have the option to move in there if you want. Demetri is engaged to your cousin, after all."

"I can't even begin to make a decision until I take a look at your facility."

"You can drive over with me now. I'll bring you back tonight."

She shook her head. "No, I'll come on my own in the morning."

"All right. This offer is a win-win situation for everyone." And, because he couldn't help himself, he placed his hand over hers. In an instant, electricity coursed from her fingers straight to his gut. Her hand twitched, as if she felt it, but she didn't jerk away.

She simply kept her eyes locked with his. "I need to think about a lot of things." She slid her hand from beneath his. "I'll go get Joe Newcomb. He'll load Something To Talk About in your trailer."

"All right."

Marcus blew out a breath as she strode off—slim legs in tight jeans and scuffed boots. He knew full well he was playing with fire. Probably destined to get singed in the process. But he didn't care.

All he cared about was having her near.

Chapter Three

After dinner, Melanie sought out her brother Brent. As was his habit most nights, he had settled at the massive desk in the second-floor study. There, he spent hours compiling information and reviewing the spreadsheets he'd created while a fire blazed in the gray stone fireplace.

As Quest's head breeder, it had been Brent who'd first learned that the routine recheck of Leopold's Legacy's DNA revealed that the Derby and Preakness winner had not been sired by Apollo's Ice, the stallion of record. Since then, Brent had spent uncountable hours trying to find out how such a disastrous mistake could have been made. And at the same time attempting to unearth the name of the horse that had actually impregnated Leopold's Legacy's dam, Courtin' Cristy.

Making Brent's job tougher was the need to balance

work with raising twin eight-year-old daughters. Cancer had killed their mother three years ago, and Melanie still questioned whether her brother would recover from the loss of the wife he considered his soul mate.

"Do you think we'll ever find out the truth about Apollo's Ice?" Nudging a stack of file folders aside, she slid a hip onto one edge of the paper-strewn desk.

Brent leaned back in his chair. A good-looking man, he was more rugged than refined and wore his dark hair a little longer than Robbie and Andrew. But he had the same blue eyes. And identical grim expression.

"Up until two months ago, I would have said yes," Brent replied. "This wouldn't have been the first time a mistake had been made at a stud farm. Most of the stallions and mares are trucked there, so the stable workers aren't familiar enough with the horses to recognize them by sight. There are usually so many mares in heat at the same time that it's always possible one could wind up being bred to the wrong stallion. Or a mare could get covered by the right stallion, but the paperwork on that covering shows a different stallion's or mare's name altogether."

Melanie nodded. She knew that at a stud farm, all horses were required to wear head collars with their names on them. Even so, it was up to the workers to check those names against breeding lists. As in any workplace, not all employees were as conscientious as others.

Brent curled his hands into fists. "My thinking changed two months ago when Dubai happened."

His tone had gone as hard as tempered steel. Harrison Rochester, an English baron, had also owned a horse believed to have been sired by Apollo's Ice. Rochester's horse had died suddenly at his stable facility in Dubai. Tests conducted on the horse's blood revealed that it had been poisoned. Equally shocking was the revelation that its sire was not Apollo's Ice, but the same mystery stallion that had fathered Leopold's Legacy.

"Anything new on the Thoroughbred Registry's computer tech who suddenly quit?" she asked, then furrowed her brow. "I don't remember his name."

"Ross Ingliss, and I still haven't been able to track him down. All I know for sure is he entered the corrupted data about Leopold's Legacy's DNA into the registry's computer system. And that his financials show he's got a lot more money than his salary brought in."

Too antsy to sit still, Melanie pushed off the edge of the desk and wandered to one of the floor-to-ceiling bookshelves.

The scent of the fire mixed with the aged sweet aroma of leather-bound books sent her back in time. As a little girl, she had loved dashing into this room to sit on her grandfather's lap at the big desk. He would spend hours regaling her with stories about horses and the daring men who rode them. Listening to him, Melanie had fallen in love with the sport of racing and set her heart on becoming a jockey. She had never been prouder than the day she first wore Quest's colors.

Now, it seemed that everything around her was slipping away. Only to herself would she admit that her heart ached with the possibility that she might never again ride for Quest Stables.

She took in Brent's bent head and the tight line of his shoulders while a sick dread rose inside her. If he couldn't find Leopold's Legacy's true sire, or if he did and that sire was not a registered Thoroughbred, the winner of two Triple Crown races would no longer be considered a Thoroughbred. Her parents would then be forced to forfeit the millions the stallion had won racing. And they would have no way to recoup that loss because his stud value would be zero.

Marcus was right, she thought. Her staying at Quest would be the equivalent of doing nothing to try to plug a ship that had sprung a huge leak. If she went to work at Lucas Racing, she could put everything she had into riding Something To Talk About to wins. Wins that would put money into Quest's anemic bank accounts.

Doing so would be a comforting solution, if she hadn't spent so much time engaging in wanton fantasies about the man poised to become her new boss.

Maybe if she hadn't purposely stayed celibate for the past two years, Marcus's kiss wouldn't have hit her like a kick from a ticked off half-ton horse. As it was, the instant he'd touched her, desires, too long untapped, had risen to the surface, drawing her into a world of steamy, potent passion. Melanie knew she could easily get lost in that world. Too fast. Too easily.

She couldn't let that happen. Refused to get involved again with a man about whom she knew so little, and who didn't seem to be willing to open up to her.

"You want to tell me what's on your mind?"

She turned, discovered Brent watching her with unwavering curiosity. "A few things."

Moving back to the desk, she leaned a hip against it. "Christmas being one. Katie and Rhea came down to the stables yesterday after school. The entire time the twins filled feed bins they chattered about the gift lists they gave you two weeks ago. Apparently they're expecting Santa—meaning you—to bring them everything on those lists."

When Brent puffed out a breath, Melanie sent him her best withering look. "You haven't even thought about shopping yet, have you?"

"I've been busy." He waved a hand toward the computer's monitor. "Things on my mind. I'll get to the shopping."

"Yeah, right." It was well-known around Quest that all three Preston brothers would rather have teeth pulled without the benefit of anesthetic than venture into a mall.

Melanie held out her hand. "Give me their lists. I've got Christmas shopping of my own to finish. I'll do yours while I'm at it."

Looking like a man who'd just received a reprieve from death row, Brent dug into one of the desk's drawers, pulled out the lists and handed them to her. "You're a lifesaver, sis. I owe you."

"Big-time. And I already know how you can repay me."

Brent's eyes turned wary. "How?"

"E-mail me all the information you've compiled since Legacy's DNA discrepancy first came up."

"Why? You think I've missed something?"

"No. It's just that up to now, all we've done is talk about things as they've come up. I'd like to read the reports you've made on all the interviews you conducted. Get a better idea of the big picture."

Brent lifted a shoulder. "Couldn't hurt to have another set of eyes look over everything."

"That's the idea." When she started to turn away, her brother snagged her arm.

"You doing okay with Something To Talk About being gone? I know he's special to you."

"I miss him." Just saying the words put a lump in Melanie's throat. She put her hand over Brent's and squeezed. "Right before I came up here, I found myself in the kitchen choosing a pear for him, like I've done every night for months. I had to remind myself that Something To Talk About wasn't out in his box, waiting for me."

"I'm sorry, Melanie. The silver lining to all this is that you know he's in good hands with Marcus."

"True." Just the mention of Marcus's name had her feeling a prick of disloyalty. "He's offered me a job."

Brent's eyes widened. "Marcus?"

"Yes. I don't want to leave Quest, but…"

"You're a jockey, who right now can't race."

Melanie nodded. "I can't believe I'm even considering going to work at Lucas Racing."

"When will you make a decision?"

"Tomorrow. I'm going there to take a look at the place." She dipped her head. "For now, this is between you and me. If I decide to take the job, I'll get the entire family together and tell everyone at the same time."

"Damn." Brent leaned back in his chair. The strain he felt from months of digging to get at the truth showed clearly in the dark circles under his eyes. "If you decide working there is the best thing for you to do right now, then that's what you should do."

"Problem is, I don't know if it will be the best thing for our family."

Brent shook his head. "Us Prestons are a tough lot, just ask Grandpa. We'll get through this, no matter what. And, in my opinion, you can't go wrong working for a trainer like Marcus. He's a natural-born horseman. The animals respond to him in that indefinable way they do to someone they feel comfortable with. Marcus'll produce champions, and you'll be there to ride them."

"Sounds like we'll make a great team," Melanie murmured. It was beyond ironic that the sum total she knew about the man who'd kissed her senseless was how he handled and treated horses. And here she was, seriously considering uprooting herself from her family's stables and going to work for him.

How, she wondered, could a job offer seem both tempting and threatening at the same time?

THE FOLLOWING MORNING, Melanie steered her vintage turquoise Thunderbird convertible over rolling hills caught in the gray haze of winter. In the distance, horses grazed, manes ruffling in the cool December breeze.

Her hands tightened on the wheel when she spotted the two stone posts Marcus had noted in the directions he e-mailed her. Squaring her shoulders, she turned and drove up the gravel lane.

When she saw the house, she braked the car to give herself time to study the structure.

In the summer the house would be shielded by the tall, massive maples that now sported only winter-bare branches. Through gnarly limbs she could see the white columns rising up from a wide covered porch and the fluid curves of the two-story redbrick house. She remembered Marcus saying that the former owners had neglected to maintain the main house. The new owners' intent to bring it back to pristine condition was evidenced by the half-dozen vans and pickups sporting names of contractors and other service companies parked along the length of the porch. Still, from where Melanie sat in her idling T-Bird, the house looked almost regal.

Knowing her cousin Elizabeth's penchant for flowers, she found it easy to picture how the landscape would look in the late spring, exploding with color.

But it was months until spring. Right now, the grounds of Lucas Racing looked as bleak as Melanie felt. Never in her life would she have imagined herself leaving her family's home and business to work for a competing stable. The fact that she was well on the way to doing exactly that had her stomach rolling while she drove the rest of the way up the drive.

She parked the T-Bird away from the clutter of trucks and vans. Sliding out, she pulled on her pale green lambskin jacket to ward off the brisk morning wind. Though her intention had been to call Marcus's cell when she arrived, she found herself setting off on her own, taking the crushed stone path that led around the side of the house.

Several outbuildings came into view. Then sheds and a barn. Farther out, where the earth curved up, she could see horses grazing and the faint glimmer of sun striking water. A few more steps and she reached the back of the house where a brick patio spilled out of tall French doors.

Off to one side sat a two-story building of the same redbrick as the house. The first story consisted of a long garage with four parking bays, their white doors closed. Glistening second-floor windows overlooked a balcony spanning the building's entire length, with metal stairs at each end.

Melanie continued along the path until she spotted two large white buildings with ventilation turrets along the roofs. Stables, she knew. Nearby was an oval track where horses and their handlers had gathered for morning exercises. Split-rail fences and paddocks checkerboarded the area and the scent of hay and horses drifted through the cool air.

Closer now to the oval track, Melanie spotted Something To Talk About, easily distinguishable by his gray coat and white stockings. Even though she'd only been away from the colt for a short time, she allowed herself a tiny spark of pure envy at seeing one of the exercise boys riding him.

Next, she turned her attention to the men standing along the fence that ringed the track. As if she were a heat-seeking missile and he her target, her gaze zeroed in on Marcus. Clad in jeans, a blue work shirt and thick denim jacket, he stood with one booted foot propped on the fence's bottom rung, his black hair glinting beneath the strengthening sun. She took in his clear-cut profile, the hard geometry of his jaw, the no-nonsense curve of his mouth.

That mouth, she thought. She knew the feel of it. The taste.

An ache settled deep inside her.

She curled her fingers into her palms. If she was going to work here, *work for him,* she had to get a grip. Lusting after the boss was not allowed.

As she made her way to the fence, five horses were loaded into a portable gate that had been positioned on the racetrack. When the last of the back gates was shut, Marcus pulled out a stopwatch. His finger flicked a switch the instant the gates sprang open.

The horses flew out.

Gripping the fence, Melanie stood transfixed, tracking the horses while they took the first turn. Nothing on earth gave her heart more of a knock than watching that first rush of speed as the blur of powerful bodies surged forward in unison.

Her throat closed, burned with a desperate need to be a part of that again. To sit astride Something To Talk About while he raced like the wind against other horses.

It was then she knew for sure she would leave Quest and work here.

Her gaze slid back to Marcus. He didn't need to know yet that she'd made her decision. She had got little sleep last night, thanks to him. But she hadn't let those hours go to waste. Instead, she'd booted up her laptop and created a strategy.

Now, she was ready to negotiate terms. And determined not to agree to work at Lucas Racing until Marcus agreed to them.

ALTHOUGH HE KEPT his attention on the track, Marcus knew the instant Melanie approached. It was as if he could scent the woman from a mile away. Deliberately, he kept his eyes focused on the horses streaking around the oval while he slammed the door on thoughts of her.

Even so, he knew it was more than just the thundering hoofbeats that had his blood drumming.

He watched the horses speed along the track, felt the earth vibrate beneath his feet as they headed down the backstretch. When they neared the finish line, Something To Talk About held the lead by three lengths.

And kept it.

"Damn good time," Marcus said after checking his stopwatch. He studied the riders rising high in their stirrups while slowing their mounts. "You get that time down, Billy?" he asked after a moment.

"Yes, sir." The head groom, a stooped, white-haired man, rechecked his own stopwatch while making notes on the clipboard he held propped on the top rail of the fence. "That colt has the thirst to race, all right. He's a fine addition to your stables, Mr. Vasquez."

Your stables, Marcus thought. For a man who'd left home as soon as he'd been able, moving from stable to stable, track to track, it was going to take time to get used to hearing those words. And to accept that, by putting down stakes, he had lost a measure of the freedom he once thought he would never willingly surrender.

But he *had* given it up, and he intended to make a success of the venture he and Demetri had embarked on. Starting with the help of Something To Talk About.

"You're right, Billy," Marcus agreed. "That colt will be Lucas Racing's first star."

If Melanie hadn't been there, Marcus would have vaulted the fence and gone to the horses to stroke them while giving the riders a comment or two on their performance. But she was there, and he'd spent a sleepless night wondering if she would take him up on his job offer. He wasn't going to keep her waiting.

While the exercise boys led the horses away to cool down, Marcus turned to her. "Something To Talk About doesn't appear to have suffered from his move here."

"He's a champion," she said, a mix of pride and pleasure in her voice. "He knows it." She paused for a moment, and Marcus caught the quick shadow that flicked in her blue eyes. "He'll win, no matter who's riding him."

"The champion part I agree with," Marcus said, studying her.

She'd clipped back her short blond hair in a way that should look messy but instead made him suspect he was getting a glimpse of how intriguingly rumpled it would be after a bout of hot sex. Beneath her pale green lambskin jacket she wore jeans and an ivory turtleneck sweater that looked incredibly soft.

Just like her skin. *That* was something he had personal knowledge of. A woman with skin like that could tempt a man until she drew him in, heart and soul.

He fisted a hand against the top rail of the fence. He would do well to remember he'd grown up watching the misery that resulted when one person was drawn to another with a strength of emotion that bordered on obsession. It was a type of fixation that stripped one's soul over time, taking away instead of giving until there was nothing left but an empty shell.

Instinct told him if he ever let loose the part of him that was never allowed out of control, he could fall that deeply, that dangerously for Melanie Preston.

So, even though there was something about her that reached out to him as a man, and begged him to conquer her as a woman, he would not allow himself to act on that desire. He would adhere to his rule of keeping his hands off coworkers.

And the sooner he convinced her to take the job at Lucas Racing, the better. "Your statement that Something To Talk About will win no matter who's riding him is debatable," he commented.

"He came in ahead of the other four horses a few minutes ago," she pointed out.

"True. But no matter how hard his rider tried to get him to stay down the middle, the colt veered toward the outside." Marcus sent her a knowing look. "Which is something I'm sure you noticed, too. By doing that, Something To Talk About had to cover yards of ground the other horses bypassed. And he ignored it when his rider tapped his flank with the crop, trying to get him to move inward."

Melanie pursed her lips. "Your new horse is an independent thinker, Mr. Vasquez."

"He's only partly my horse, Miss Preston. And he doesn't think independently when *you're* on his back. I've seen you ride him in person and I've studied videos of you on him during workouts and races. He pays attention to your signals and acts on them. When you're in the saddle, it's all fluid, flawless teamwork."

Her focus shifted to the far end of the track where the colt was being led to the stables. "He and I have this communication thing going. He listens to me, I listen to him."

"Keep it up because whatever you say to each other works." Marcus slid his stopwatch into the pocket of his denim jacket. "Do you want to tour the stables and other buildings first? Or would you rather see the quarters you'll have if you take the job?"

"The stables." She patted her right hand against her jacket pocket. "I brought a pear for Something To Talk About."

"Then let's go give it to him."

BY THE TIME MARCUS had shown her through the stables, the barn and the offices, the sun had warmed the air enough that Melanie had shed her heavy jacket and carried it draped over one arm.

"From what I've seen, you have the makings of a first-class facility," she said while they headed up the crushed stone path toward the big house.

"It will be. After Demetri's renovations are finished on the main house, the place will be top-notch. Unfortunately, that's going to take a while."

"Speaking of Demetri, where is he?"

"Rome. Elizabeth's doing a couple of concerts in

Italy. Apparently he can't go for more than a few days without seeing your cousin."

"True love," Melanie said and smiled. "I got an e-mail from her saying they're trying to schedule a wedding date for next year between her tours." While they continued up the path, Melanie swept a hand toward a mass of flower beds. "By then, Elizabeth will have had all these beds planted. It'll be gorgeous around here when everything blooms."

Marcus paused at the edge of the brick patio and turned to face her. "Will you be here with me to see all those flowers?"

Melanie felt a flutter in her stomach. She knew exactly how she would like to be *with him.* Down, girl, she told herself.

"That depends," she said evenly.

"On?"

"Three things."

"I'm listening."

"When we went through the stables, you outlined a few renovations you and Demetri plan to make. I'd like you to agree to three more."

She saw caution kick into his dark eyes. "What sort of renovations?"

"As you know, I've been studying new stable management theories. One being how important it is to pay attention to the flow of energy."

Marcus's brow furrowed. "How exactly do you do that?"

"By placing doors and windows in the right orientation."

"That's the only theory you've been studying?" he asked neutrally.

"No, color," she said. "Horses don't see color the way we do, but they can differentiate various hues. Everything in your stable is painted a dingy gray. It's depressing, to people and horses. Also, there's no music."

Marcus stared at her for so long that Melanie felt the urge to squirm. Then he gripped her elbow and nudged her along the path that led to the two-story brick building she'd noticed earlier

"There are two apartments on the upper level," he explained. "If you take the job, the one on the south will be yours."

"Who lives in the other one?"

"I do."

Side by side, they headed up one of the building's gleaming white staircases. Melanie didn't ask if he intended to agree to the changes she'd suggested for the stables. Patience, she told herself as they stepped onto the wooden balcony that spanned the building's front. She would find out soon enough.

Marcus slid a key into the lock of the nearest door, swung it open. "I realize this is much smaller than you're used to, but it's nice."

She stepped past him into a bright, cozy room with pale yellow walls and a shining oak floor. A tan leather sofa and matching chair sat in front of a small brick fireplace. Melanie could see rambling hills through the wide sheer-draped windows.

New, top-of-the-line appliances sparkled in the kitchen. A tub with jets took up one corner of the tidy bathroom. The walls of the bedroom were painted a pale blue; sheer white curtains hung at the two windows. The soft blue and white were repeated in the bedspread, and a round rug spread a pool of color on the wooden floor. A framed mirror hung over the whitewashed pine dresser.

Marcus had remained in the bedroom's doorway, one shoulder propped against the jamb. She met his gaze in the mirror. "These quarters are more than nice."

"Glad you think so. You said your taking the job depends on three things. You told me one. What's another?"

"For the past five years, I've sponsored a summer mentor program for students. I'd like to continue it."

Their gazes were still locked on each other's mirrored reflection.

"I worked at Quest this past summer," Marcus said. "I don't recall your program."

"I put it on hold this year." Her chest tightened at the thought of how many things the DNA discrepancy had touched. "I was busy working with Robbie, trying to get Something To Talk About up to speed."

"Which you did," Marcus acknowledged. "A lot of stables use working students during the summer. In exchange for all the chores they do, they get riding lessons and room and board. Is that the type of program you're talking about?"

"No. The kids I work with all want to be jockeys and their riding skills have to already be at a certain level. I give each student a one-on-one inside look at a jockey's life. We work on their form, I teach them signs to watch for while they're riding that might indicate a horse has an injury. And what to look for in a horse's performance so they can tell the trainer what's going on." Melanie pursed her lips. "That would benefit you."

In the mirror, she watched Marcus push away from the door and move toward her. With every step he took, her pulse beat faster.

"What's the third condition on your taking the job?"

Here we go, Melanie thought. To buy time, she laid her folded jacket on top of the dresser while she tried to remember her carefully constructed reasons against their further personal involvement that she'd come up with during the sleepless night. Sleepless because of him.

She turned, and discovered he now stood only inches from her. Close enough to make her feel threatened. And tempted.

While the incredible scent of musky aftershave and potent male surrounded her, *aroused her,* she decided in retrospect that a bedroom probably wasn't the prime place to have this conversation. Especially since her thought processes had suddenly detoured into wondering how it might feel to toss caution aside, shove him onto the bed and have her way with him.

Which she absolutely, positively was not going to do, she lectured herself. A reminder of the battering her heart had taken by another man who'd shared nothing about himself was all it took for Melanie to square her shoulders and dive in.

"What happened between us in your office at Quest can't happen again."

"The kiss, you mean?"

Had his voice actually softened, or was she just imagining that? "Yes. If we're going to work together, we need to agree on that."

"It won't happen again," he said levelly. "I keep my hands off my coworkers and employees. That's an unbreakable rule as far as I'm concerned. Does that take care of your concerns?"

"Well." Melanie blew out a breath. Apparently she was the only one having lust control issues. "Yes, that covers everything," she said, hoping she sounded as casual as he did.

"Then we shouldn't have any problem if you decide to take the job." He raised a dark brow. "Are you going to take it, Melanie?"

He was the most compelling man she'd ever met. His black-as-midnight hair and eyes, the olive cast of his skin that made her think of the time she'd spent racing in sunbaked Spain, his chiseled mouth and strong jaw—they were an absolutely riveting combination.

Which made working with him a huge complication. One she would have to deal with in order to help her family's precarious financial situation.

She angled her chin. "Are you going to agree to my ideas for the stables?"

"After you explain them to me in depth, I'll consider them."

"Fair enough. What about my mentor program?"

"You've got the go-ahead on it. I want to sit in when you interview each student."

"Agreed."

"So, what about the job?"

"I'll take it." Automatically she stuck out a hand.

Marcus's gaze flicked downward, then rose slowly to meet hers. "Remember what happened the last time we shook hands?"

Thoughts of that torrid kiss shot heat straight up Melanie's spine. Flexing her fingers, she lowered her hand to her side. And pasted on a cool smile.

"According to Spanish custom, we sealed our friendship."

His answering smile was not much more than a faint curve of his mouth but there was an intimate, knowing quality to it that sent a frisson of excitement along every nerve ending in her body.

He crossed his arms over his broad chest. "So, tell me, friend, when do you want to start work?"

"Tomorrow. I'll go home now to tell my parents and grandfather that I'm coming to work for you. Then I'll pack my things."

"All right." He glanced at his watch. "I need to get back to the stables."

"I'd like to look around here again and make some notes on how much storage space is available. I'll lock the door behind me."

She waited until Marcus strode out of the room, then turned to collect her jacket off the dresser.

Working with the man was *not* going to be a problem, she told herself. Because she wouldn't allow it to be.

Melanie glanced into the mirror and stared at her reflection. "Liar," she whispered.

Chapter Four

Marcus stood outside the stables in the crisp morning air and checked his watch. The driver of a trailer delivering a bad-tempered filly had phoned to let him know he was five minutes away from Lucas Racing. Marcus wanted to be present when his newest pupil trotted down the trailer's ramp.

Out of the corner of his eye, he caught movement in the distance. The sky was sparkling clear, the sun fully lifting just above the horizon as Something To Talk About soared over the ground with Melanie on his back. She sat in the saddle as though she'd been born there, her movements in perfect sync with the horse's. This, Marcus knew, was strength and beauty. Magic in motion.

The rare times she wasn't riding, schooling or racing something with four legs, she turned her attention to other tasks. She'd already compiled figures and submitted spreadsheets to him on her mentor program for the upcoming summer. Then there was the blizzard of memos that had hit his desk detailing the cutting-edge stable management techniques she thought had merit. She performed all those tasks with enthusiasm, but riding, Marcus knew, was her passion.

Every other morning, she raced Something To Talk About on the oval track with the other horses Marcus had in training. On the off mornings, she saddled the colt and took him out to streak like a silver rocket over the fields and gentle slopes, going to the far boundaries of the property.

A week had passed since she agreed to work for him. Seven days during which he had steadfastly kept his focus on the duties of his own job. Lord knew he had plenty of responsibilities to keep him busy throughout each day.

His nights, however, had turned to hell.

It was then that he lay staring at the ceiling, imagining Melanie in her own bed just feet away in the apartment on the other side of the wall. He wondered what she slept in. *If* she slept in anything. Or was she snuggled under the blankets, naked on the opposite side of that Sheetrock barrier?

He was driving himself slowly mad, but he couldn't stop thinking about her. Couldn't rid his senses of the taste of her. The scent.

Couldn't stop wanting her.

Through narrowed eyes, he tracked the gray colt as it cantered into the paddock, watched her bring one slim leg over the saddle, then vault lightly to the ground with a smooth grace that could only come from years of experience. She handed the reins to one of the stable boys, who led the colt away to cool off and be groomed.

Marcus knew the moment Melanie became aware of him. Her chin came up and a sudden tension seemed to settle in her shoulders.

It was the same strain he'd sensed in her that day in her bedroom when she brought up the strike-you-blind kiss they'd shared. He had news for her—just because he'd agreed to keep his hands off her didn't mean he had moved on from thinking about that kiss. Imagining it.

And wanting it to happen all over again.

He watched her cross the paddock, bend through the fence rails, then head his way. The female sway of hips beneath butt-hugging jeans had his heart picking up speed.

"Morning," she said, peeling off her leather gloves.

"Morning." The scent of her—soap and cool skin—stirred every hunger he'd ever known. "Enjoy your ride?"

"Always." When she shoved her fingers through her short hair, the sun picked up its blond highlights. "Lucas Racing is drawing attention."

"From?"

"Observers. I saw a couple of them parked on the public road at the east edge of your property." She tipped her head in the direction she'd ridden in from. "Both had high-powered binoculars."

Observers, Marcus knew, were employed by racing columnists who relied on their reports for information and tidbits to fill their pages. This month, with most everyone's mind on the holidays and no races being run, the observers were looking under rocks for stories.

"Mark my word, there'll be a column in tomorrow's paper about Lucas Racing." Melanie stuffed the fingers of her gloves into the back pockets of her jeans. "Demetri's fame as a race driver adds to the cachet of his partnering with one of the best horse trainers in the country." She slid Marcus a look. "Maybe in the world."

"Then there's the ace jockey who rode the winner of this year's Derby and Preakness races and recently left her family's stables to work here," Marcus added. "All that ought to be worth a couple of columns."

"True."

Just then, the throbbing of an engine drew Marcus's attention. He turned in time to see a pickup towing a horse trailer roll slowly along the drive.

Melanie glanced at the trailer. "Are you adding another horse to your training schedule?"

"A filly." Marcus nodded at Billy, the white-haired head groom who had headed up from the stables. "Her owner refers to her as a volcano waiting to erupt. I've been hired to deal with her aggression issues."

"Aggression issues," Melanie repeated. "In other words, she's mean."

"And runs like hell when she makes up her mind to do it. Unfortunately for her owner, that doesn't always coincide with the days the filly is scheduled to race. I understand she likes to toss off jockeys just to see them fly into the air."

"Does she?" Melanie lifted a brow in subtle challenge. "You're going to let me ride her, right?"

Marcus hesitated. He'd worked with other female jockeys and never had a second thought about putting an experienced woman rider on a horse with behavior problems. But suddenly, he felt an overwhelming protectiveness toward Melanie. He didn't want to think about what the falls and horses' hooves could do to all that soft skin.

Or what *she* would do to *him* if she had any idea what he was thinking.

"I want to work with the filly for a couple of days on my own," he answered. "You can ride her after that. Then tell me if she makes any sort of subtle moves right before she tosses a hundred-pound jockey out of the saddle."

"She might not have any luck pitching me off. And you know where to find me when you're ready for me to climb on her."

Did he ever, Marcus thought. Especially at night.

In silence, they watched the tall, lean driver and young groom climb out of the truck. The trailer's loading ramp rattled as the groom lowered it, then he disappeared inside. Minutes later, he led the filly down the ramp.

She was black as pitch with a blaze like a lightning bolt down the center of her forehead. Her ears were laid back and her dark liquid eyes looked murderous. Studying her, Marcus furrowed his brow. The filly's gait was more of a bad-tempered stalk than a trot.

"She doesn't look like she wants to make new friends here," Melanie murmured. "What's her name?"

"Who's Cheatin' Who?" Marcus answered. "Her owner named her not long after she caught her husband in bed with his secretary. The wife took him for everything he had, including ownership of several Thoroughbreds."

"So, maybe this filly is just overly cranky because Mom and Dad got a divorce?"

The filly's apparent response to Melanie's question took the form of a lowered head and arched back, and a kick like a bronco's.

While the groom clamped both hands on the reins to gain control, Marcus stepped toward the filly.

"Be careful, sir," the groom said. "She's guaranteed to nip you a good one. Especially if you turn your back on her."

Marcus acknowledged the warning with a nod, then put his hands on either side of Who's Cheatin' Who?'s head. When he locked eyes with the filly, he felt a quick, hot thrill race through him at what he saw. Malice. Rebellion. Ferocious pride. The key would be to teach her to take commands without damaging that wild spirit.

"So, you bite *and* kick, do you?" he asked while running a palm along the muscled neck and shoulder. Beneath his hand he felt power. Energy. "No matter," he murmured. "You and I are going to get along just fine."

The filly snorted.

Deliberately, Marcus turned his back, and as she lifted her head, he glanced over his shoulder. "Not a good idea," he warned softly. They eyed each other another moment, trainer to pupil, then Who's Cheatin' Who? tossed her head in the equine equivalent of a shrug.

Marcus thanked the groom and the driver, then slid a look at Billy. "You can take her now. Get her settled in her stall. I'll be down in a short while."

"Yes, sir."

While the driver helped the young groom slide the trailer's ramp back up, Melanie stepped to Marcus's side. "Before you get busy with her, I need to ask a favor."

Turning, he caught her cool scent and felt his hunger stir all over again. "What?"

"I plan to go into town this afternoon and buy a few Christmas decorations. The trunk of my car is so small it'll hold only a couple of shoe boxes. If it's okay, I'd like to borrow one of the stable's pickups."

Giving her a considering look, he crossed his arms over his chest. "Does buying Christmas decorations have anything to do with your ebb and flow ideas about the stables?" As he spoke, the trailer's engine started, then the heavy vehicle rolled slowly up the drive. "If so, I don't want to walk in there tomorrow and find all the horses wrapped in twinkle lights while carols play in the background."

She gazed up at him through her lashes. "There's only one small thing I plan to hang in the stables. You have my word it isn't twinkle lights. The other stuff is for my quarters."

"Then you can borrow a pickup. Billy has the keys."

"Thanks. Have fun with the filly," Melanie said, then headed up the drive.

Although he needed to get to the stables, Marcus stayed where he was, watching her go. Just the sway of her hips had him whistling through his teeth.

"Hell," he muttered and scrubbed a hand over his face. He might as well accept he had a lot of sleepless nights ahead of him.

IT WAS DARK by the time Melanie parked the pickup in front of her quarters. She'd be the first to admit she had gone overboard buying decorations. Way overboard. But, dammit, this was her first Christmas season away from home, and a girl was entitled.

Her parents had been totally supportive when she told them she was leaving Quest to go to work for Marcus. Her grandfather and her brothers had agreed she'd made the right decision. Still, knowing her family understood her reasons for leaving home didn't make her miss them less. In fact, homesickness had settled so hot and heavy in her belly it ached. She hoped that bringing some of her family's Christmas traditions to her new digs would lessen that ache.

She bundled shopping bags into her arms and slid out of the pickup into the chilly night air. Hauling the groceries and decorations she'd bought up the stairs to her apartment was a cinch. It was the five-foot Douglas fir in the back of the pickup that would require some serious muscle.

The hulking fir that matched her own height was the same type of tree that always stood in the conservatory at Quest. December after December.

She had just made her third trip up the stairs and returned to the pickup when the sound of footsteps caught her attention. Peering through the evening gloom, she watched Marcus stride up the drive under a cold slice of moon, his tall form silhouetted against a row of spindly trees.

Her throat went bone-dry. He looked good. Damn good. Tall, dark and at ease with his surroundings. The silver light and shadows made him appear a little dangerous. A whole lot desirable. As if he'd just climbed out of bed.

Melanie clamped her jaw tight. She had no idea what the man looked like when he climbed out of bed—or into one for that matter—and the last thing she needed was to start imagining Marcus Vasquez anywhere near a mattress.

When he came alongside the pickup, he scowled. "Is that a six-foot fir in the back of my pickup?"

"Five foot." She slid her sweaty palms down her jeans. "I sort of got carried away."

"Where are you planning on putting it?"

"In my living room." She raised a shoulder. "I was just about to head down to the stables to see if some of the hands will help me lug it in."

"They're busy doing evening stables right now."

Without another word, Marcus lowered the pickup's tailgate and hefted out the fir.

"Wait!" Melanie grabbed the tree's top branch as it slid out of the truck bed. "You can't do that by yourself."

"I'm doing it," he said through gritted teeth.

He certainly was, she thought, appreciative that there was sufficient moonlight for her to see his muscles bulge beneath his tan sweater.

Getting a firm hold on the top of the tree, she took the lead, guiding him up the stairs and into her apartment.

"It'll be fine," she said, after Marcus positioned the fir in the stand she'd bought. The tree took up an entire corner of her living room, but Melanie didn't care. She needed some Christmas cheer.

After tugging off her coat, she started digging through the numerous sacks she'd piled on the floor. "I can't believe I bought so much stuff," she commented while pulling out boxes of lights, silver ornaments and tinsel.

"Enjoy," Marcus said, then turned toward the door.

"If you help decorate, I'll reward you when we're done." She didn't give the statement any thought until she saw him halt midstride and turn slowly back to face her.

"A reward?" he asked softly, one of his dark brows sliding up.

Oh, boy. "I bought cookies and the ingredients to make hot chocolate." The heat pooling in her cheeks told her she was blushing like a schoolgirl. "Having snacks after the tree trimming is a Preston family tradition."

Marcus studied her while she went back to rummaging through the sacks. After a few minutes, she pulled out a pink box with the name of a local bakery scrawled across the top. "See? Chocolate chip."

He didn't give the box a glance. Instead, he kept his eyes focused on the woman with blond hair the shade of polished gold, and features that were more interesting than striking.

Just looking at her had need rising like a warm wave inside him. He knew the smart thing to do would be to tell her he'd see her in the morning, then head to his own apartment next door. But tonight, her blue eyes seemed almost too bright and her enthusiasm over decorating the tree carried an edge he couldn't ignore.

He glanced at the boxes she had opened and spread out on the coffee table. All contained silver ornaments.

His mind scrolled back to the huge Christmas tree in the conservatory at her family's house. The tree loaded with white lights and silver balls.

"You're homesick," he said quietly. He had never experienced the emotion himself, yet he recognized it in her. Maybe because he had lived around her family and had witnessed the love they shared for each other.

Melanie hesitated, then nodded while she pried open a box of lights. "I'm that transparent, am I?"

"I'd say it's more that I'm learning to read you."

"Scary," she murmured while edging behind the tree. She plugged in the strand of twinkling white lights and began threading it through the branches. "It's Christmas. I miss my family."

"You're entitled." Marcus took the loop of lights dangling from her hand and wove them across the front of the tree, then handed the remainder of the string back to her on the other side.

"Most people my age moved out of their parents' home long ago," she said while they added more lights. "But with the stables there and me eventually becoming the main jockey for Quest, it just made sense to continue living at home. Same thing goes for my brothers since they all work for the family business, too."

"I imagine they miss you as much as you do them."

Her mouth curved. "Nice of you to say."

"I'm not being nice. It's a fact."

"Right. I'll try not to accuse you of being nice again, Vasquez." She eased out from behind the tree, retrieved a box of ornaments and handed it to him. "We've got the lights done, time for the fun stuff."

Marcus felt his chest tighten against the brush of her fingertips. "I was wondering when we were going to start having fun."

He had never considered trimming a tree "fun." Mainly because his childhood memories of Christmas included the bleak depression his mother always sank into. Watching her spend each December quietly miserable had left him with an instinctive dread of the holiday season. She had been dead ten years, and he knew by now he should have shrugged off that baggage from his childhood. Instead, it had dug its claws in and stuck with him, so he'd simply opted to avoid all things Christmas.

Until tonight with Melanie.

Mulling that over, he began hanging ornaments on the upper branches.

An hour later, with white lights, silver ornaments and tinsel glinting in the fir's branches, he settled on one end of the couch, Melanie on the other.

"We did good," she observed, sipping hot chocolate. "Thanks for the help."

"Don't mention it." Marcus sampled his own hot chocolate. "The reward's not bad, either." He studied her for a long moment. She looked more at ease now, yet there was an emotion in her eyes he couldn't define.

"Does having the tree take the edge off being homesick?" he asked.

"It helps."

"Look, I know you're planning to go home for your dad's birthday party on the twenty-third, then stay over for Christmas. If you want to go before then, it's fine with me."

She studied him over the rim of the mug. "Are you

forgetting you entered Something To Talk About in Florida's Gulf Classic Race on New Year's Day? And that I'm riding him?"

"I seem to recall that."

"The more he and I work together, the better our chances at winning. And I want to win, not just for Lucas Racing but for my family. They need the money their shares in the colt will earn."

She rubbed at the center of her forehead as if an ache had settled there. "I just hope that before Christmas, Brent can find some answers to all the questions about Leopold's Legacy's lineage. That would be the best present my family could receive."

"Has anything new come to light?"

"No. It's all just fresh in my mind because I've spent the past two nights going over the spreadsheets and reports Brent's compiled. I've made notes, tried to look at things like a cop would, hoping to spot something Brent missed."

Marcus set his mug on the coffee table. "No offense, but do you really know how a cop looks at things?"

"I once dated a homicide detective."

Marcus caught the expression that crossed her face, a quick shadow as she placed her mug beside his, then shifted back on the couch.

There was something still there, he thought. Hurt?

"Must have been interesting," he murmured.

"Interesting, but a huge mistake. The good news is that he liked to talk about the best way to conduct investigations."

"For example?"

"Say the cops have a series of murders they believe were committed by the same suspect. The cops know to pay a lot of attention to what happened during the first killing. That's because it's generally handled carelessly. Murder is like everything—practice makes perfect. So the first one is sometimes sloppy, hasty. Forensic evidence is often left by the suspect. With each murder that follows, he learns to be more careful. Perfects his skill, so to speak."

"What does a serial homicide investigation have to do with Leopold's Legacy's DNA?"

"Maybe nothing. But I keep going back to where everything began."

"The Angelina Stud Farm," Marcus said. "Which is not far from Quest."

"Right. Nearly five years ago, that's where Apollo's Ice covered a number of mares, including Leopold's Legacy's dam. Several people witnessed their mares breeding with Apollo's Ice, but DNA from the foals born eleven months later prove that Apollo's Ice didn't sire them."

Marcus nodded. He had spent hours contemplating what had occurred behind the scenes after those matings. "Have you found something in the spreadsheets that Brent overlooked?"

"No. As far as I can tell he's turned over every stone trying to find out what happened. He even flew to England to interview Nolan Hunter, the owner of Apollo's Ice." Melanie stared at the Christmas tree for a moment, then shrugged. "Hunter has some sort of royal title, but I don't remember what it is."

Viscount Kestler, Marcus answered silently while a chill ran up his spine. Up until ten years ago, he hadn't known his father's identity, or that he even had a half brother and sister. After he'd learned the truth, he'd had one encounter with Nolan Hunter. His half brother had displayed a vicious side that, if made public, Marcus was sure would curdle the blue blood of every proper English royal.

"Brent told me about his trip to see Hunter," Marcus said carefully. "Your brother believed Hunter's claim that he doesn't have any idea how things could have gone so wrong at the stud farm. Do you agree?"

"Yes," Melanie answered. "After all, Hunter was in England when it all happened. He sent one of his grooms with the stallion, and the groom stayed with Apollo's Ice the entire time he was at stud."

"Another dead end," Marcus said.

"Which is what Brent keeps running into everywhere he looks. But something went on at that stud farm and someone out there knows the truth. Uncovering it might be the only hope of saving Quest."

Marcus thought about how lonely and bitter his mother had ended up. On her deathbed, she had exacted his promise to never reveal the name of the man who had fathered him, then rejected them both.

The promise to his dying mother was ample reason to keep the truth about his connection to Nolan Hunter to himself, Marcus reasoned.

But even as he assured himself of that, a wave of guilt ate through his gut like acid. It didn't matter that he had nothing to feel guilty about. He respected the Prestons, had done what he could to try to help ease their financial burden. He had no proof his half brother had anything to do with the breeding fraud. Yes, he loathed Nolan Hunter, but Marcus acknowledged his feelings were colored by the cruel way Hunter's father—*his* father—had callously cast off his mother. And himself.

He turned to look at Melanie. She seemed lost in thought while she studied the tree, its lights and ornaments glittering. He wanted to touch her, brush away those lines of worry that were haunting her eyes. *Haunting him.*

What would she do, he wondered, if she learned his connection to the owner of the horse that had tarnished her family's reputation and put their livelihood in jeopardy? Even though Hunter hadn't been implicated in foul play, would she decide working for the man's half brother was a little too close for comfort and leave?

Marcus felt the jolt, the flash of awareness that came with the possibility of her walking away from Lucas Racing. *From him.* It wouldn't just be one hell of a jockey that he lost. But a woman who was beginning to matter.

A lot.

Chapter Five

The following afternoon, Melanie balanced on a step-ladder while tacking a sprig of mistletoe topped by a red bow over the door to Something To Talk About's freshly painted stall. When a deep voice boomed out, she nearly fumbled her hammer.

"What does someone have to do to get attention around these stables?"

"Grandpa!" Grinning, she scrambled down the ladder, stepped into Hugh Preston's arms and kissed him lavishly on both cheeks. "What are you doing here?"

"Since when does an old man need a reason to visit his only granddaughter?" he blustered, enveloping her in a fierce hug.

"You're not old." Just the scent of his familiar spicy

aftershave helped ease Melanie's homesickness. "Everybody knows you'll live forever."

"That's the plan." He was a big man with gray hair and white brows over sharp blue eyes. At a hearty eighty-six, he still traveled to local races and placed bets on horses running at tracks all over the world.

"Living forever will allow me to continue reading about my famous granddaughter, the jockey." A crafty gleam settled in Hugh's eyes. "Who has recently abandoned the family homestead to go to work for a pair of young, upstart stable owners."

Not until her grandfather glanced toward the stall across from them did Melanie realize Marcus was nearby. Dressed in jeans, a maroon shirt and denim jacket, he rested a forearm on the top of the stall door. Peering around her grandfather's arm, she watched Marcus's gaze slowly rise to the mistletoe. When he looked back at her, it was as if his dark-as-midnight eyes touched her face with a hot, melting awareness.

She felt a bump under her heart, and a quickening of her pulse. "It's tradition," she explained, hoping the heat flooding into her cheeks hadn't turned them scalding red. If the man thought she was hinting to get kissed again, he was mistaken.

And if she told herself that enough times, she might begin to believe it.

"A tradition at Quest," she clarified. She looked back at her grandfather, trying to ignore all the heated signals passing between herself and Marcus. "Grandma Maggie always hung mistletoe in the stables at Christmas, didn't she?"

"Always, she never missed a year," Hugh said with a wistful smile. "My Maggie would be proud to know you're carrying on the tradition."

"It seems the Prestons have a lot of family traditions," Marcus commented.

"We do." Hugh surveyed the nearby stalls, then furrowed his forehead. "But none that come even close to painting the inside of the stables blue."

"A first for me, too." Marcus glanced into the stall nearest him. "I have to admit the colors seem to have a calming effect on several horses. Maybe I should consider the paint job a tradition for Lucas Racing?" he suggested just as the heavy tread of boot heels announced the approach of one of the stable boys.

From the corner of her eye Melanie watched Marcus turn. With his attention shifted, she studied his face. The little spike of lust that shot through her at the thought of their kissing under the mistletoe she'd hung didn't count, she decided. After all, they had agreed not to lock lips again. Ever.

She had a flash of memory—her body pressed intimately against Marcus's, his mouth ravishing hers….

When her pulse picked up speed, she shook her head and dropped that line of thought like a stone. Allowing herself to relive those crazed couple of minutes was the last thing she needed.

"Grandpa, did you read something new about me?" she asked, switching mental focus.

He nodded. "In this morning's newspaper. I spotted the column the minute I turned to the sports section. It talked about you moving from Quest to Lucas Racing.

The author described how fit Something To Talk About looks, and speculated on his chances of winning the Gulf Classic Race on New Year's Day."

"I haven't seen the paper yet." Melanie replaced the hammer she still held in the small toolbox she'd borrowed from one of the farriers. "I imagine the information came from observers. I saw a couple of them the other morning when I was out schooling Something To Talk About."

As if on cue, the colt stuck his head over the stall's half door.

"There's the silver bullet." Grinning, Hugh shifted, ran a palm along the length of the long, muscular neck. "Those observers the columnists hire don't miss much," he said while the horse butted his head playfully against Hugh's shoulder. "Since the day Maggie and I brought the first Thoroughbred to Quest, there have been observers with binoculars dotting the side of the public roads like trees. They watch the horses. The jockeys. They know when a trainer gets fired, which usually results in a horse being moved to a different stable. Some observers get so good they know every horse by sight. A remarkable feat, considering that young horses alter shape as they develop month by month."

Hugh dug a sugar cube out of a pocket of his tweed jacket and offered it to the colt. "Observers, and that invisible network that exists among workers at various stables, are why secrets don't stay secrets long in our close-knit racing world."

For no logical reason, her grandfather's last statement caused a little twinge at the base of Melanie's spine. She looked at Marcus to find him watching her with something in his eyes she hadn't seen before. Shadows. Secrets.

Her stomach did a roller-coaster dip.

Which was ridiculous. She already knew the man was obsessively closemouthed. He didn't talk about his past. Didn't say much about the present. And if he had plans for his future, he didn't share them.

That was his right. He didn't owe her any explanation about his personal life.

But she'd been hurt and made a fool of by a man who had had one hell of a secret. So she wasn't about to ignore that what she saw in Marcus's eyes was something more than just a penchant for privacy. It was unmistakable guilt that flickered an instant before he looked away.

He's hiding something.

Just then, Marcus gave the stable boy a nod and stepped toward Hugh. "I'm sorry I can't spend more time with you. The owner of a pair of horses I'm training just showed up and I need to meet with him."

"Of course." Hugh offered his hand. "You've got to take care of business," he agreed. "I'm grateful you called. I appreciate you doing that."

"Don't mention it." With that, Marcus turned and strode down the concrete floor that separated the rows of stalls.

Melanie looked at her grandfather. "What did he call you about? And when?"

"Marcus phoned early this morning." Hugh fondled the colt's muzzle, and the horse blew contentedly down its nostrils. "He told me you were missing your home and family."

"Oh, jeez." She closed her eyes for a moment. "My boss called my grandfather to tell him I'm homesick."

"I view Marcus more as a former employee of Quest with whom I developed a mutual respect." Hugh gave her cheek a gentle pat with his huge hand. "I'm grateful for his call because the truth is, I've missed you something fierce. Been pondering driving over and paying you a visit. After Marcus phoned, I decided there was no time like the present, and had one of the grooms bring me over."

"I'm glad you came." She glanced in the direction Marcus had gone. "Grandpa, what do you know about Marcus?"

"Well, now." He paused, his gaze somber as he regarded her from his towering height. "I don't think you're asking what I know about his past jobs."

"No, that's all in the résumé Andrew has on file at Quest."

"You want to know my opinion of what kind of man he is, right?"

"Yes. No." She shoved a hand through her short blond hair. "I just think there's something in Marcus's past he's keeping quiet about."

"He has a right to his privacy, Granddaughter. Just like you."

"I know. You're right, I should just leave things alone." And stop thinking about him in any capacity other than her boss. Not going to happen, she knew.

Hugh reached out, wrapped his hard, calloused hand around hers. "No matter what's in his past, Marcus is a caring enough sort to call an old man to tell him his granddaughter's missing her family. To me, that speaks volumes about his character."

Melanie squeezed his hand. "I keep telling you, you're not old."

"Right. So, how about showing me where you're living these days?"

"Sure." She resolved to enjoy her grandfather's presence, no matter how he came to be there. "I just got my Christmas tree decorated last night."

Hugh lifted a silver brow. "Did you keep to the Preston tradition? Chocolate chip cookies and hot chocolate after the tree trimming?"

"Of course." She tilted her chin his way. "I've got leftovers, too."

"Then it sounds like you have all you need to make yourself feel right at home."

She nuzzled her cheek against his shoulder. "I do now."

THE FOLLOWING MORNING, Melanie walked through the soft gray dawn into the stables, where the scent of hay and horses hung in the chilly December air. The first thing she heard was Marcus's deep voice.

"If you want to be a groom, Ken, you have to work with all the horses. Even the bad-tempered ones."

"Yes, sir. I know. I'm just getting geared up for this one. She gives moody a new definition."

Inside the stall, the young groom, bone-thin with spiky red hair, stood gritting his teeth and rolling his shoulders. Marcus held Who's Cheatin' Who?'s reins with one hand while he stroked the lightning blaze down her nose.

"Good morning," she said, taking in the black-as-coal filly's laid-back ears. "Apparently, Lucas Racing's newest student is in her usual foul mood."

Marcus nodded, his expression set. "She hasn't gotten it through her thick skull yet that I won't put up with that mood."

The sleeves of his denim shirt were rolled up, and the muscles in his forearms tightened as he gripped the reins. Standing there in form-fitting jeans and well-worn boots, his coal-black hair mussed, he was a picture of hard-edged, physical competence.

Just looking at him made Melanie's mouth water.

Ken shot a wary glance at the horse. "It doesn't much matter what mood she's in," he mumbled. "This one doesn't like me a bit."

"You're making a mistake by letting her know she intimidates you," Marcus said. "She has to be groomed like every other horse at Lucas Racing. That's your job. Do you intend to do it, or not?"

"Yes, sir, I do."

"Then get on with it."

A little too quickly, Ken turned toward the kit holding grooming brushes. Melanie opened her mouth to warn him to be careful just as Who's Cheatin' Who? bunched, then kicked out.

Swearing, Marcus shoved Ken aside with his shoulder and took the hoof in the ribs. The air turned ripe with a string of curses.

Without a second thought, Melanie eased into the stall, a knot in her throat. She laid her hand over Marcus's on the reins to help control the filly.

A half ton of horse struggled against them. Melanie

felt the heat from the filly, and from Marcus when their bodies knocked together. "How bad did she get you?" she asked, keeping her tone even.

"Less than she would have liked," he gritted out, pain thickening his voice while he muscled the filly down.

"I'm sorry, boss," Ken said, his eyes anxious. "I guess I moved too fast."

"You should have more sense than to turn your back on a bad-tempered horse," Marcus rasped. "Go on, now, she got the best of you and she knows it." He glanced at Melanie. "Give us some space, okay?"

"Your ribs—"

"Will wait."

While Ken disappeared through the stall door, Melanie backed toward it. Silently, she watched Marcus jerk the reins enough to bring the filly's head down. If the movement jarred his ribs, he didn't show it.

"If you don't want to run in races, then I'm wasting my time with you." As he spoke, Marcus kept his dark eyes locked with the horse's belligerent gaze. "Would you rather I tell your owner to put you out to pasture to breed? I do that, you'll wind up standing around all day, never knowing what it's like to run. To win."

Marcus kept his voice hard, and Melanie understood that he knew there was no way of cajoling this particular horse with sweet words, encouraging pats, tugs on the ears. A battle of wills was what the filly sought, and that, from Marcus, was what she would get.

His tactic seemed to be working. Who's Cheatin' Who? stood quiet now, her ears at attention, her dark molten eyes no longer exuding a challenge.

Marcus flicked Melanie a look. "Come back in," he said, his voice remaining even. "Talk to her while she gets your scent. Then we'll saddle her."

Melanie slipped back into the stall. "You want me to ride her now?"

"If you don't, she'll know all she has to do is throw a demonic fit and she gets left alone."

"We need to get your ribs checked," she murmured as she took the reins. With her free hand, she rubbed the filly's neck, her side.

Marcus took a step back. "She barely got me."

"I saw the kick you took, Vasquez. It was a hell of a lot more than barely."

"You want to ride this filly, Preston? See if you can stay in the saddle of a horse that's tossed off too many jockeys to count?" One of his dark brows lifted in subtle challenge. "Or maybe you know that's exactly what will happen. So you've decided to play it safe, become a nursemaid to a trainer who took a little tap from a horse's hoof."

Melanie flashed him a narrowed look as she continued stroking the filly's neck. "I'll make you a deal, Vasquez."

"I'm listening."

"I'll ride this bad girl and stay on her back until *I* decide it's time to get off. After I'm done, I get to take a look at your ribs, tough guy. Deal?"

"Deal."

MELANIE STAYED IN THE SADDLE.

Barely.

"Tell me about the ride," Marcus said while a groom

led Who's Cheatin' Who? away, her black coat glistening with sweat.

Walking side by side, he and Melanie headed into his tidy, oak-paneled office at one end of the stables. He knew he was going to have to stick to the damn deal he'd made about his ribs, but first he wanted Melanie's report on the filly's performance.

"She was mulish and reluctant so we got away slowly from the starting point." Melanie pulled off her riding helmet and shoved her fingers through her short blond hair. "Which I'm sure you saw," she added.

"I saw," Marcus commented while he swung the office door shut. He'd seen, too, a stunning picture. The long-legged Thoroughbred with her regal head and gleaming black coat, and the slender woman riding her around the oval track.

"When we reached the backstretch, she gave two of her bronco kicks." Melanie took a seat in a chair while Marcus leaned against the front of his desk. "To her credit, there aren't too many horses who can manage that while running full out."

Marcus scrubbed his hand across his jaw. "No, there aren't." Like all trainers, he depended on an experienced jockey's analysis of how a horse acted on a racetrack, which might—or might not—be what he'd trained the animal to do. For that reason, this type of briefing was invaluable. "Go on," he urged.

"On the next turn, she put her head down and arched her back." Pure appreciation settled in Melanie's blue eyes. "I'm not sure how she managed to do that maneuver, either, but it's a move almost guaranteed to send a jockey flying."

"You stayed on her," Marcus pointed out. He'd held his breath while he watched through binoculars, knowing it had taken skill and a remarkable effort of balance on Melanie's part to pull herself back up into the saddle from somewhere below the filly's right ear.

"I stayed on her barely, and I'm not too proud to admit that," she said. "Who's Cheatin' Who? didn't toss me because instinct told me she was getting primed to pull some sort of trick. If I hadn't been waiting for it, she'd have sent me over the fence."

Marcus shifted, tried to hide a grimace when his bruised side protested the movement. "I've got a lot of work facing me with that filly."

"Which ought to pay off in the long run because she's a powerful runner." Melanie pursed her lips. "But you've got something different facing you right now, pal."

"My ribs," he grated.

"Your ribs," she confirmed and rose. "So let's have a look. And I'm warning you, if you've got a cracked one, I'm driving you to the doctor."

"I don't need a doctor."

His comment earned a look of eye-rolling exasperation. "You sound like my brothers. Tough guys, all of you. But your bones are just like anyone else's. They get hit with enough force, they break."

He crossed his arms and stared down at her. "You don't have an M.D. after your name. There's no way you're going to know just by looking if I've got a cracked rib."

"I'm a jockey." She drew in a deep breath that

Marcus noted had an interesting effect on her breasts beneath her slim red sweater. "Falls, bruises, concussions and broken bones are part of my job description."

"I've got work," he stated, forcibly lifting his gaze and focusing on her face. *She's an employee*, he reminded himself. *Don't think about what you'd like to do to that sexy body.* "We can do this later."

"We made a deal, Vasquez." She planted her hands on her hips. "You either pull up your shirt, or I'll do it."

"Dammit to hell," he muttered, and jerked his shirttail out of his jeans. He would have told her she was wasting his time, but the movement had his entire side throbbing like an abscessed tooth.

When she got a look at his side, her eyes widened. "My God, Marcus, you said she barely got you."

"I'm fine."

"So, your definition of 'fine' is having a saucer-sized bruise that makes your side look like a piece of rotten fruit?"

"Sounds about right," he muttered, then grunted when she pressed her fingertips at the edge of the bruise. "They're sore, all right?" he hissed. "I don't need you poking around."

"I'm sorry, but I meant what I said." She leaned in, her face inches from his side, as if she had X-ray vision and could see through his skin. "The least you can do is let me drive you into town so a doctor can look at you."

"I don't need a damn—hell!" He clamped a hand on her wrist to keep her from pressing the bruise again. The motion brought her inches closer. All at once, Marcus became aware of the intense feminine scent of her perfume, her heat. Looking down, he traced her profile with his gaze, the curve of her cheek and jaw, the corner of her mouth.

The mouth he lay awake nights thinking about kissing again.

Heat swarmed into his blood, and suddenly he was dealing with an entirely different kind of ache.

He sucked in a breath between his teeth. "I've had a few cracked ribs in my time, so I'd know if I had one now." It took a Herculean effort, but he managed to keep his voice even against the pain. "I don't. It's a bruise, Dr. Preston, and after all your poking and prodding it's throbbing like a son of a bitch."

"I'm just trying to…"

Her voice trailed off when she straightened. He was still leaning against the desk, not standing at full height so their mouths were now only inches apart. Marcus could read the nerves in her eyes as clearly as he could see their vivid blue color.

He felt the heat already teeming in his blood ratchet to blast-furnace intensity.

Melanie's breathing hitched while her body stiffened against the warmth that rushed over her skin. She was aware—too aware—of the pressure of his fingers locked around her wrist. When her mind shifted to wondering how those firm fingertips would feel skimming against her flesh, she took a step backward. Then another, and tugged from his hold.

"Well, if you're sure your ribs are okay." She

pushed at her hair and discovered her hand wasn't quite steady.

"I'm sure." When he jerked down his shirttail, he winced.

Which helped get her mind off the way her knees had gone weak. "At least take something to dull the pain."

"That I can agree to. I've got some over-the-counter stuff in my apartment."

She glanced around the small office. "You don't have aspirin or anything here?"

"There's a bottle of scotch in the bottom drawer of my desk. I use it to seal deals with owners of Thoroughbreds, but right now a stiff shot ought to hold me."

Glad to put some space between them, Melanie stepped behind the desk. "Why not sherry?" she asked while retrieving the bottle of scotch and a glass from the drawer. "When I rode in a couple of races at the Mijas Hipodromo, all the local jockeys bragged that Spain has the best sherry in the world."

With his back still to her, Marcus rolled a shoulder. "I'm only half-Spanish."

She could tell by his voice that the comment had been an aside, given with little thought. But to her, it was the first crack in the wall he kept around his personal life.

"Really?" she asked idly while pouring two fingers of scotch into the glass. "What's the other half?"

He was momentarily still. Then he straightened, turned and faced her across the desk. "Horse trainer," he said, his expression impenetrable.

Melanie's eyes didn't leave his. "Anything else in that mix?"

"Nothing worth mentioning."

She started to ask questions, to push, but there was something in the black depths of his eyes, a No Trespassing sign that warned her to back off, that had the words turning to dust on her tongue. And anger surging through her.

"Fine." She thumped the scotch bottle down on the desk. "You don't want to tell me anything about yourself, that's your business."

"Not much to tell."

A vicious case of frustration had her fisting her hands. "You know what? I heard that exact line from the homicide detective I dated."

"The cop who gave you tips on how an investigation works?"

"One and the same. He never had much to say about himself. Didn't talk about his past, present or future. But I was so crazy about him, I overlooked that. Figured he had a right to his privacy."

"Doesn't everyone?"

"When keeping quiet about things doesn't hurt someone else. Problem is, the cop didn't talk about his personal life because he had a wife at home he conveniently forgot to mention. A *pregnant* wife."

"Ouch."

"Exactly. So, you'll understand that I'm a little wary of men, women—*anyone*—who, for whatever reason, share nothing about themselves."

Marcus kept his dark gaze locked with hers, and remained silent.

Melanie saw now, though she told herself she didn't

care, that there were places inside him no one, no woman, would ever touch.

The fact she was one of those women had hurt slicing through her anger.

She stalked around the desk, grabbed her helmet off the chair. "You don't want to talk about yourself, fine. It doesn't matter, after all, since we agreed to keep things between us on a boss-employee level."

"Melanie—"

"You cheated," she tossed out.

He frowned. "What?"

"You cheated by calling my grandpa and telling him I was homesick. That's not something a boss should do."

"I thought we were friends, too." His voice was husky. Low. "Or have you forgotten that night at Quest when we sealed our friendship?"

She swallowed against the knot of desire that settled deep in her belly. "I'm not forgetting anything, especially what I know about friends. They share things about themselves. They trust each other. You've chosen not to do either. *Your choice,* Marcus. That means all you are is my boss. Period."

Jamming her helmet under one arm, she jerked open the door. It swung closed behind her, the flat sound broken by the echo of her boot heels on concrete as she stalked away.

It wasn't just her words that had every muscle in Marcus's body clenched tight, but the scent she'd left behind. The perfumed mix of roses and sunshine mingled with the creamy fragrance of her skin in a way that made him feel drunk just inhaling it.

Resisting her was like trying not to breathe. The magnetism he felt toward her was undoubtedly sexual. But it was more than that.

Stronger even than lust.

That knowledge terrified him right down to the marrow. Almost as much as the thought of her learning the truth and walking away from him and Lucas Racing.

He swept the tumbler off the desk, tossed back the scotch. Its slick, smooth taste hit his gut like a hot fist.

Frigging hell, up until ten years ago he hadn't known who his father was, hadn't cared. When circumstances forced his one meeting with the bastard who'd sired him, and the half brother he hadn't even known existed, Marcus vowed to never again have any contact with either man.

Several years later, when he happened to glimpse a newspaper article about the death of his blue-blooded father, he'd felt nothing.

He had felt plenty, however, when he learned Nolan Hunter, his half brother, owned Apollo's Ice, the stallion at the center of the Prestons' problems. That knowledge had been one reason Marcus had ended his employment at Quest. The Prestons' finances were another. Their reputation in the racing world had taken major hits, and the entire family could lose their home, their livelihood.

Jaw set, Marcus splashed more scotch into the glass, drank it down.

Melanie was all about family. The only reason she'd left Quest and come to work for him was to race Something To Talk About. Successful finishes on the Thoroughbred ensured that the Prestons earned money off the shares they still owned in the colt.

The throb in Marcus's ribs intensified as he moved behind the desk and settled into the chair. He considered pouring himself another shot of scotch, then decided against it. Numbing his brain with alcohol wasn't going to get him anywhere. Leaning back, he closed his eyes and forced his mind to work beyond the pain.

He disliked his half brother intensely, but that was due to the cold, heartless way the Hunters had treated his mother. That Nolan Hunter was a jerk with a fancy title didn't mean he'd engineered the scandal that centered around his stallion. Still, there was no proof Hunter *wasn't* involved. If it turned out he was, it would be only a small mental step for people to wonder—they couldn't help but wonder—if his half sibling had his hand in that scandal, too. After all, it was because of the Prestons' misfortunes that Marcus had wound up part owner of his own stables. And his first acquisition had been the colt the Prestons had hoped would be their saving grace.

Yes, people would wonder about that.

Melanie would wonder. The thought that she might suspect his actions had helped put her family teetering on the edge of ruin tightened the knots already in Marcus's gut.

She would leave Lucas Racing and him.

And, why, he asked himself, would it matter so much if she did?

Businesswise, he knew the answer. She was one of the best jockeys he'd ever worked with. Her winning races for Lucas would bring in more business. Up profits.

Emotionwise was an entirely different matter. It was the intensity of his need for her that had him skittish. A need that went beyond a desire to toss her on the nearest surface and take her. Claim her. His hands hurt from wanting to touch her. Just touch her. And it damn well didn't help to know that she tasted as delicious as she smelled.

Don't go there, Marcus told himself. He'd made a promise to his mother never to tell anyone about his past. It was a promise he intended to keep. And because he could not be forthcoming with Melanie, that meant she was off-limits.

"Boss, employee," he muttered. That's all he and Melanie could be.

Maybe all they'd ever be.

Chapter Six

The mingled smells of hot horse and cold morning mist filled Melanie's lungs. She could hear only the swish and thud of galloping hooves. With her booted feet firmly in the stirrups, she lay almost flat along Something To Talk About's withers, reveling in the feel of crisp wind and the lash of the colt's mane against her face.

His muscles strained for more speed as he sprinted over the grassy field at the western boundary of Lucas Racing's property. Melanie sent up silent thanks to the stable's previous owners. They had neglected a lot of areas of maintenance, but not this field. It had been continuously maintained at racecourse flatness, so there was no danger of a galloping horse encountering uneven ground.

If only she could keep riding this way, forever and

ever, she thought. But fences and walls seemed to be everywhere in her life. Fences of the mind, of the heart.

She spurred her mount still faster, as though through speed she could outrun the self-directed anger and hurt that had plagued her since she'd stalked out of Marcus's office the previous day.

Hadn't she known better than to get starry-eyed over a man who kept information about himself under wraps with a depth of secrecy the CIA would envy? To do so was the equivalent of a guaranteed trip to heartbreak. And to wallow in hurt over his refusal to give her even a small glimpse of what was behind that controlled exterior of his was a brainless waste of emotion.

Which was *her* problem, she lectured herself for the hundredth time. She knew everything necessary in order to work for Marcus. In truth, her respect for him had grown tenfold in the short amount of time since she'd signed on at Lucas Racing.

It hadn't taken her long to understand that Demetri Lucas was the ultimate silent partner. The sleekness and slickness of the operation were due solely to Marcus's expertise. Already the horses under his charge were on the way to being well-schooled and beautifully turned out. She had seen nothing makeshift or second-best in any aspect of the young business. Its potential for success and prosperity was evidenced in the facility's ruthless cleanliness, the top-notch tack. And he had this grassy exercise field inspected every day. Even the crimson horse rugs with *LR* monogrammed in glistening silver thread spoke of quality.

Then there was Marcus's patience and dedication to

the horses, his understanding of their moods and pref-
erences, and his genuine affection for them. Except for
her family, Melanie had never been involved with a
man who understood the hard work, the disappoint-
ments, the sweat and bloodletting of the horse-racing
business.

Dammit, she wasn't involved with one now! She
was simply in…major lust mode. Dealing with a
hormonal heat surge after two years of sexual drought
couldn't help but keep her on edge and put a hair trigger
on her temper. With time, the fire inside her would
subside, then eventually go out, so she just had to wait.
Meanwhile, she would make sure there were no more
Christmas decorating sessions with the man. Or any
other off-duty activities.

As an insurance against temptation, she resolved
to take down the mistletoe the minute she got back
to the stables.

While Something To Talk About galloped across a
stretch of property in sight of a public road, Melanie
glanced over her shoulder. Sure enough, two men stood
beside a parked car, binoculars focused her way. It never
took long for observers to learn the exercise routines of
horses that were considered serious contenders in
upcoming races. The sportswriters they reported to used
miles of newsprint to analyze a horse's overall record
and its potential in order to advise bettors of the pros
and cons of briefly aligning their future with a certain
Thoroughbred.

On impulse, Melanie leaned closer to the colt's right
ear. "How about we give those observers a show? Let

them know you're the guy to beat in the Gulf Classic on New Year's Day?"

Just as she was about to give the horse free rein, she heard her name shouted over the thunder of hooves.

A figure darted from a shadowy thicket of trees.

Melanie had a split second to recognize Carl Suarez, a teenager who'd worked in her mentor program at Quest the summer before last. His sudden appearance, complete with arms waving like a flagman signaling the start of a race, sent Something To Talk About swerving sideways. And rearing up.

The quick lurch caught Melanie by surprise. She tumbled out of the saddle and landed on her behind with a stunning thud against the hard ground.

Her first reaction, after her head stopped spinning, was astonishment that she had fallen at all.

Next came a slash of fear that Something To Talk About's jerky moves might have injured one of his front legs.

Luckily, she still gripped the left rein in her fisted hand. She scrambled to her feet, yanked off her helmet and dropped it to the ground.

"It's okay," she told the colt, forcing a calm into her voice she was far from feeling as he skittered sideways.

The sound of the teen calling her name again as he approached only made the horse more jittery.

"Stay back, Carl!" she hissed over her shoulder. "You know better than to startle a horse like that. What the hell are you doing here?"

"I'm sorry. I don't... I need... God, Melanie, I need help."

Only then did she register the tears and the panic in his voice.

"Just hold on," she said, softening her tone. "You can tell me why you're here after I check my horse." Tightening her hold on the reins, she knelt down and ran her free hand along the colt's forelegs.

"Okay, but hurry. Hurry."

Carl's words, sounding as if they were a breath away from hysteria, made Melanie's throat go dry. Something had to be terribly wrong for him to show up out of the blue. How had he known where to find her? And why did he feel the need to talk to *her* when they hadn't seen each other in a year and a half?

Relieved that the delicate bones in Something To Talk About's front legs felt normal, she straightened and rubbed his muzzle.

"It's okay, big guy," she soothed, keeping her gaze on the huge brown eyes that still reflected a thread of distress. "This is Carl Suarez, he joined my mentor program before you were even born. He wants to be a jockey and ride amazingly handsome horses like yourself."

The colt shook his massive head, his bit and bridle clinking with the movement.

"How about you get in a little grazing time while Carl and I talk?" she asked, leading the horse to a grassy area almost completely enclosed by saplings. She didn't tether him to one of the trees—that would ensure broken reins and jab the bit down on his mouth. But the circle of young trees would create a sort of corral while he grazed, which he could do, despite wearing the bridle.

After a few moments of watching him munch grass

peacefully, Melanie strode back toward Carl. She was well aware the observers were still standing on the road. Tomorrow's trade papers would probably carry all the details of her tumble out of the saddle.

Can't do anything about that, she thought, then focused her full attention on the cause of that fall.

Carl Suarez was short, slightly built, with dark hair and the beginning shadow of facial hair that marked the slide from adolescence into manhood. A silver ring pierced his left eyebrow. She remembered him as a teenager full of youthful enthusiasm. The young man wearing only blue jeans and a black T-shirt who stood shivering in the cold December morning looked as though he'd aged a decade since she'd last seen him.

"Carl, what's wrong?" Without waiting for an answer, she pulled off her quilted jacket and wrapped it around his shoulders. "Why are you here?"

"My dad's dead!" he blurted. "He's dead."

Stunned, Melanie could only stare at him for a moment, before she forced her brain back into operating mode. Years ago, Carl's father, Santos, had been a groom at Quest. He'd quit to take a job at the Angelina Stud Farm.

"I'm so sorry, Carl. When…?"

"Last night!" he said, his voice cracking with emotion. He was trembling harder now, his entire body shaking. "God, he's dead. Dad's dead. I ran. I just ran."

At a total loss, Melanie gripped his hands and found them as cold as ice cubes. "Ride back with me to Lucas Racing. We'll get you warm, and you can tell me—"

"No!" His hands tightened on hers. "He tried to shoot me, too, but he missed. He'll still be looking for me."

His words zinged her heartbeat to frantic. "Your father was *murdered?*"

"Yes!"

"The police…. Did you call them?"

"No. I have to get out of town. Help me, Melanie. Please."

"I will," she assured him. Although at this point she had no clue how. "If you won't come back to the stables with me, let me call my boss, Marcus Vasquez. He'll drive here to meet us. We can sit in his car while you tell me what happened. It'll be warm in the car."

"No! I don't know your boss." Carl's hands tightened on hers with bone-cracking intensity. "I know you. I *trust* you."

"Then believe me when I tell you that you'll be safe with Marcus."

"No one but you!" Carl's eyes were saucer-wide, his lungs heaving. "If you call him, I'll take off."

"Then I won't call Marcus." So much for bringing in reinforcements, Melanie thought, and dragged in a shuddering breath. She was on her own, the equivalent of groping her way through the dark.

"You need to tell me about last night, Carl. You have to start at the beginning and tell me everything. Then I'll know how to help you." At least she hoped so.

He gave a jerky nod. Tears gleamed in his red-rimmed eyes. "Okay."

"Let's get you off your feet." She tugged him toward the stand of trees, nudged him down to sit against a sturdy maple.

"You're freezing," she said. "Slide your arms into my jacket and button it."

"You're cold, too."

"I've got an insulated shirt on under this heavy sweater, so I'm fine." She watched him fumble his arms into sleeves that were inches too short for them. He made an attempt at closing the jacket's top button, but gave up when he couldn't control his trembling fingers.

"We'll get you through this," she said quietly while reaching out and securing the buttons. "Start at the beginning. Tell me everything."

He drew his legs up, wrapped his arms around his knees. "My dad and me, we've been having trouble. He's been on my case about stuff."

"Such as?"

Carl pointed an unsteady finger at the silver ring in his left eyebrow. "This. And he didn't like some of the friends I made at school this semester. But I got the feeling it wasn't just things I did that had him so freaked-out." Carl shrugged. "We just fought a lot."

Melanie had a vague memory that Carl's mother died when he was an infant. And that he was an only child. "So, you and your dad have been at odds," she prodded.

"Totally. After school yesterday I went to the mall with a friend. I had to buy Dad's Christmas present." Carl squeezed his eyes shut. "Dad picked me up at the mall. He acted different."

"How?"

"Sort of calm, or something. And he had a weird look on his face. He handed me the sports section from the newspaper. It had a column about you."

Melanie nodded. It was probably the same one her grandfather had mentioned. "Did your dad say why he wanted you to see the column?"

"No. All he said was it wasn't right that you'd had to leave your home and go to work for some other stables. That you belonged at Quest. He talked about how your family had been real good to him when he worked there."

Carl tightened his arms around his knees. "Dad said he knew the truth about what went on at the stud farm when that stallion, Apollo's Ice, covered a bunch of mares."

Melanie's spine went stiff. Santos Suarez had been a trusted employee at the Angelina Stud Farm for years. The prospect of finally learning who was behind the fraud that had brought her family to the brink of ruin put a river of heat under her skin.

"My brother Brent told me he talked to your dad a couple of months ago," she said evenly. Brent had spent weeks tracking down and interviewing everyone he could find who'd worked at Angelina when Apollo's Ice was there. "If your dad knew the truth, why didn't he tell Brent?"

"He told me he kept quiet because they threatened to hurt me if he didn't do what they wanted him to."

"Did he say what that was? And who 'they' were?"

"No." Despite the thickness of her heavy jacket, Carl's body trembled. He paused as if to gather his thoughts.

"Last night in the car, Dad said he'd heard about a horse in Dubai that got poisoned and died. He didn't know the horse's name, just that its dam was one of the mares Apollo's Ice covered. It was all a sham, though, because the horse in Dubai hadn't really been sired by Apollo's Ice. Everyone just thought it had been, like your family's horse that won this year's Derby and Preakness."

Leopold's Legacy. Melanie curled her fingers into her palms. "So, hearing about the horse in Dubai made your dad decide to tell the truth?"

Carl nodded. "He was afraid more horses registered as foals of Apollo's Ice's would get killed. He said he had evidence to prove what went on at Angelina, and he planned to take it to the police in the morning—*this morning.* He said he'd make sure the cops agreed to protect me before he told them the truth."

"What truth?" Melanie asked quietly. "And what was the evidence?"

"I don't know. But someone at the stud farm must have figured out Dad had decided to take the evidence to the cops. He was about to tell me everything when a car sped up behind us. We'd turned off the interstate, and the road we were on was dark. All I could see was head-lights. First, I thought the car was going to pass us. Then its front bumper slammed into our car. It hit us twice that way. Dad shoved his cell phone into my hand and told me to call for help. A second later, our car skidded off the road. Next thing I knew, some man jerked open Dad's door. He shot Dad. Just shot him in the head."

A ragged keening sound escaped Carl's lips. Then he dropped his head onto his bent knees and began to sob.

"I'm sorry." Melanie squeezed her eyes shut. She felt both cold and numb, and faintly sick. *Get a grip,* she told herself after a moment. The grief surrounding the teen was like a force field, flowing off him in waves. He needed her strength, her compassion. Later, she would deal with her own emotional horror over the images his story had lodged in her brain.

Reaching out, she took one of Carl's hands in her own. While he sobbed, she did a visual check of Something To Talk About. He continued his contented grazing. The observers remained at the side of the road.

After a while, Carl's racking sobs abated. His tears lessened.

"Did you get a look at the man?" she asked quietly.

"No." Tugging his hand from hers, he scrubbed his damp cheeks. "He had on a black ski mask." He paused, stared into the distance. "I've got this slo-mo image in my brain. The car door swings open and the dome light flicks on. The guy's hand comes up. He's wearing a black leather glove. There's a space between the top of the glove and the cuff of his coat. I spot a tattoo on the inside of his wrist the instant before his finger squeezes the trigger. My dad's head…"

Melanie settled a hand on his arm. "Tell me what you did after you jumped out of the car."

As if to dispel the image, Carl stabbed his fingers through his dark hair. "I ran. It was dark, I tripped. Stumbled. The whole time I could hear shots, feel bullets whizzing by me. There were trees. I ran into the trees and hid."

And saved your own life, Melanie thought. "Why didn't you call the police?"

"Like I said, Dad and I haven't been getting along. We fight…*fought* a lot. Last week, we were in a pizza place and he started hammering me about how I need to keep my bedroom neat, help clean up around the house. Lame stuff like that. And he hated this." For the second time, Carl pointed to the silver hoop in his eyebrow. "Really *hated* it." Regret flooded his face. "I should have trashed it."

"You couldn't have known what was going to happen," Melanie reminded him.

"At the restaurant, I got so mad, I shoved Dad. Nearly knocked him down. I told him I had a right to do what I wanted." Tears welled again. "Everyone there saw how I treated him. If I go to the cops, they might think I'm the one who shot him."

"No." Melanie tightened her hold on his arm. "That's the last thing the police will think. Carl, we have to call them. They need to know you're all right. You have to tell them about the man who shot your father. About his tattoo. Did you get a good enough look at it to describe it?"

"A rectangle. Half red, half gold."

"That could help the police identify the killer."

"I'm not eighteen yet. If I go to the cops, they'll put me in some home."

"You don't have any other family?"

"Only an aunt in Mexico. When I jumped out of the car, I left my coat, my backpack. My phone, money and ID are in it. I need money to get to Mexico. That's why I'm here. I thought maybe you'd loan me enough to make it there."

"I'll help you, Carl, you have my word. But I need to ask, why me? It's been a while since we've seen each other."

"I know." He gulped in a deep breath. "I doubt I'd have thought about you if Dad hadn't shown me that column. After…while I was hiding, I kept thinking about you. The newspaper talked about the new stables you'd gone to work for. It also said you exercise the colt near this road most mornings. I figured I'd be safe coming to you 'cuz no one would expect me to do that. If the bastard who killed my dad asked around, nobody would even think to say that I knew you."

"You're probably right," she agreed. "But you live close to Quest, which is an hour away. How did you get here?"

"I snuck back to the interstate, hitched a ride at a truck stop. The trucker let me off about a mile from here."

"You spent the night out here in the cold, waiting for me," she concluded. "Carl, you need food, rest and warmth. Come back to Lucas Racing with me. You'll be safe there. I'll call my family's attorney. He'll contact the police for you. He can arrange for them to get hold of your aunt in Mexico. We'll make sure you wind up with her instead of some agency here."

"No! The killer might find out. Somehow he must have found out my dad was going to go to the police, and he'll know if I do, too." Carl surged to his feet. "I need to disappear. *Now.* If you won't help me, I'll find someone else."

In his ravaged face, Melanie read all the tearing, savage pain of a tragic loss less than a day old. She knew he was running on pure adrenaline. Knew, too, that short of wrestling him to the ground and hog-tying him—which she had no hope of doing—there was no way to make him go with her if he didn't want to.

"Just hold on." She rose, stabbed her fingertips into the pockets of her jeans, pulled out some crumpled bills. "Forty dollars is all the cash I have on me."

"It'll help."

"Take this, too." She gave herself a moment to regret the loss of the solid gold watch her family had presented her after she rode Leopold's Legacy to wins in the Derby and Preakness. Now, with the uncertainty over the stallion's lineage, those first-place finishes would probably soon be wiped off the record books, along with her name.

"You can sell the watch. Hopefully get enough cash to get you to your aunt." She forced herself to concentrate on the details of his run to the border. "You said your dad gave you his cell phone. Did you still have it when you ran from the killer?"

"Yeah, but it's broken." He shoved a hand in his back pocket, pulled out a phone. "One of the times I fell, I smashed it against a rock. It doesn't work."

"Then take mine." She unclipped the phone off the waistband of her jeans and handed it to him. "The main number for Lucas Racing is programmed into the contact list. I want you to promise to call me often. If you need help, I'll get it for you."

"I will. Thanks."

She stopped him when he started to unbutton her jacket. "Keep it. I just remembered that I stuck a PowerBar or two and a pear in the pockets this morning before I left my apartment. And gloves," she added.

"Okay."

She tightened her fingers on his sleeve. "I have to call

the police when I get back to the stables. They need to know you're not physically hurt. And hear your description of the killer's tattoo. It might help identify him."

She paused, her thoughts a jumble. There was so much raw anguish in Carl's face, she wasn't sure he even comprehended what she said. The absolute helplessness of not knowing what to do had her adding, "I'll call you if the police find the man. He won't be a threat to you then."

The teen closed his eyes, his shoulders slumped. "I hope you're not mad that I came to you. I just didn't know where else to go."

"I'm not mad." She gathered him into her arms, felt him tremble against her. "I only wish you would come back to the stables with me."

"No." He stepped away, swayed.

"Carl—"

"Gotta go." Before she could protest, he turned and dashed toward the trees.

Melanie waited until he was out of sight, retrieved her helmet, then walked back to Something To Talk About. Gathering the reins, she pressed her cheek against his strong neck for an instant, then climbed into the saddle.

With every second that passed, her fear for Carl's safety intensified like something damp and heavy, sinking into her bones.

STANDING NEAR THE ENTRANCE to the stables, Marcus handed his head groom a manila envelope. "This is the paperwork on the gelding that's due for delivery sometime this morning."

His voice was nearly drowned out by the thud of hammers, buzz of saws and whir of drills. Marcus glanced up the drive where the massive, two-story brick house stood. Each day it seemed the drone of tools increased, and he couldn't help but wonder if the renovation and refurbishing Demetri ordered would ever end.

"I told Ken to staple a metal plate with the gelding's name to a head collar," Billy Tate said. "It'll be ready to put on him when the trailer gets here."

Dressed in a faded denim jacket and jeans, the groom slipped the envelope beneath the papers on his clipboard, his rigorously brushed silver hair glinting beneath the midmorning sun. He ran an arthritic finger down the to-do list he habitually kept as the top page of his clipboard. "Guess we've covered everything for now," he said.

"All right." Employees like Billy were worth their weight in gold. Which was why Marcus had e-mailed Demetri the previous evening to let his partner know they were giving their head groom a raise for Christmas.

The crinkles at the corners of Billy's eyes deepened when he glanced past Marcus's shoulder. "Melanie's on her way back. Good, I was beginning to worry."

Frowning, Marcus turned in time to see Something To Talk About gallop into the paddock. Melanie leaned in the saddle, tossed the reins to the stable boy who jogged up to meet her.

"Why were you worried?"

"She's been gone longer than usual."

Marcus jerked his head back toward Billy. "Why didn't you tell me?"

Marcus didn't realize his tone had sharpened until one of the man's silver brows winged up.

"Well, now, I tend to get unsettled whenever any of our horses and riders are out of my sight," the groom explained. "That's the mother hen in me." He slipped the clipboard under one arm. "Melanie's an expert horsewoman. She had her cell with her when she rode out, so I figured if she had a problem, she'd have phoned."

Billy paused while he studied her. "Seems to me she had a heavy jacket on when she left, but I could be wrong." Shaking his head, he looked back at Marcus. "You want me to start telling you anytime I think a rider's been gone too long while exercising a mount?"

"No." *Just her,* Marcus thought broodingly. A day had passed since she'd left him in his office, nursing a bottle of scotch and ribs that ached like a tooth headed for a root canal. Since then, all interaction and conversation between them had been restricted to business. Boss and employee.

Physically, his ribs still throbbed when jostled. Mentally, he was on a slow ride to crazy. It had been so simple at first, when there'd been only heat. Or he'd been able to tell himself that's all there was. But *caring* for her made it all a study in frustration. And didn't do a damn thing for his business skills, either.

"No," he repeated. "You don't need to report to me about how long each rider stays out. You do a good job, Billy. I'm not going to start stepping on your toes."

The man nodded, satisfied. "I'll go file the gelding's paperwork in your office."

While the groom strode away, Marcus turned back to the paddock, watched Melanie lift one leg over the colt's neck and drop to the ground. He frowned. Even from a distance, he could tell the dismount wasn't her usual graceful springy move. And the way she shot toward the stables like a sleek bullet was anything but normal.

Concern built in his chest while his long-legged stride took him toward her. He reached the entrance to the stables at the same time she did.

Reaching out, he snagged her elbow. Up close, he saw that her cheeks were colorless, her face taut with strain. "What's wrong? What happened?"

"I need..." Her lungs heaved. "The phone. I need to use the phone in your office."

"Billy's in there." Marcus glanced at the waistband of her jeans. "Where's your cell?"

"I gave it away." Her voice sounded like rusted metal. "I need to call the police."

Every protective instinct inside him reared up at the thought someone had accosted her. "Are you all right? Did someone hurt you? Try to?"

"Not me, Santos Suarez." Her hands shook when she unhooked the strap on her helmet, jerked it off. "Someone murdered him."

"Who is Santos Suarez?"

"The father of a teenager I mentored last year at Quest."

"This morning?" Marcus asked, her words shooting a jolt of adrenaline into his system. "Did you see him murdered while you were out riding?"

"No." She pressed her fingertips to her temple. "This whole thing has scrambled my brain so I can't seem to think in a straight line. I need to calm down. Give me a minute."

"I'll wait." And while he did, he performed a slow survey of her. Her pale-as-boiled-egg skin and trembling hands seemed to be the only physical things wrong with her. Her heavy green sweater and snug jeans showed no sign she'd been in a struggle. Or witnessed a murder.

With slow deliberation, she lowered her hand. "When Something To Talk About reached the western edge of the property, Santos's son, Carl, darted out of the trees. That spooked Something To Talk About. He reared up so suddenly, I fell off."

Marcus furrowed his brow. "You're sure you're not hurt?"

"Positive. I can't say the same for Carl. He's grief-stricken. Frantic. He told me his father was murdered last night in front of him."

Marcus's jaw tensed. "Does the kid know the killer?"

"No." She pulled her bottom lip between her teeth. "And he's too scared to call the police, so I'm going to. Then Brent. I need to talk to him, too."

"Why call your brother about this?"

"Santos worked at the Angelina Stud Farm. Last night, he told Carl he knew what happened with Apollo's Ice, and he had evidence to prove it. He planned to take it to the police this morning. But then their car got forced off the road and some man shot Santos."

"Jesus." Marcus felt a prickle at the back of his neck and for an instant wondered if his half brother—the owner of Apollo's Ice—had been involved in the man's murder. All because Marcus felt... What? A deep dislike for Nolan Hunter. That hardly made the man a killer.

Digging his cell phone out of his shirt pocket, Marcus shoved away that thought and focused on Melanie. "Where's Carl now?"

"He ran off," she replied, her voice brimming with helplessness. "I tried to get him to come here, but he's afraid the man will find him and kill him, too." She held out a hand. "I'll try to explain things better to you after I make the calls."

"Hold on." Marcus glanced around. A string of horses had just been ridden in from an exercise session. Nearby, stable boys and grooms went about their work. He'd only processed parts of Melanie's story, but he had heard enough to know the information ought to be kept quiet, at least until the police interviewed her.

"You don't need an audience when you make those calls. Let's go to your quarters."

She nodded. "Probably a good idea."

Marcus hit the cell's speed-dial button while they walked side by side up the drive. When Billy answered he said, "I've got something I need to take care of. Go ahead and deal with the gelding when the trailer gets here."

With the sounds of construction filling the air, Melanie made the call to 911 while they stood on the balcony outside the doors to their respective apartments.

Marcus noted the slight quake in her hand when she

returned the phone. "Thanks. I'll wait out here so the police will know where to find me." She gave him a slight smile. "I'm keeping you from your work, and that's not good. I can deal with this, Marcus. You don't need to wait with me."

Her dismissal shot a quick lick of temper into his system.

"I'm not your boss right now, understand?" He kept his voice low, his tone even. "I'm a man who cares." *And he was about a half second away from pulling her into his arms,* he acknowledged while watching the cautious speculation his words put in her blue eyes.

"I have no doubt you can handle things," he continued. "But, right now you're upset, with good reason. So I'm staying with you until I know you've got your feet back under you."

Because he couldn't help himself, he reached out, tucked a wave of blond hair behind her ear. He forced his hand not to linger, not to slide against the soft flesh of her throat. "Got that?"

"Yes." Her eyes stayed fixed on his as color flooded her cheeks. "It's crystal clear."

Chapter Seven

Standing beside Marcus on the balcony outside her apartment, Melanie sent up a silent prayer that her legs would continue to hold her.

She had assured the 911 dispatcher she would wait outside so the police wouldn't have to hunt for her when they arrived at Lucas Racing. She wasn't, however, focused on the impending visit by law enforcement. Her legs had turned to jelly moments before when Marcus tucked a strand of hair behind her ear while murmuring he cared for her. The gesture had been so slow, so painstakingly intimate that it verged on erotic.

Her fingers tightened on the balcony's wrought-iron railing. With the scent of musky aftershave and potent male surrounding her, ninety-nine percent of her thoughts had zinged back to that night at Quest when Marcus kissed her blind.

While the strident sounds of construction hammered and shrieked from the big house across the drive, her breath caught on a surge of abrupt, intense yearning.

No, Melanie cautioned, even as the silken threads of desire tugged her toward him. It didn't matter that a heady anticipation had snapped her throat shut when he nudged that stray curl behind her ear. Didn't mean a thing that she *longed* to feel his calloused fingertips against her flesh again.

That he could melt her like a candle under the summer sun didn't change the fact he hadn't been open with her from the start. And even after she told him about the hurt she'd suffered in the past, he had made no effort to lower the walls that kept him so totally out of reach on so many levels.

Watching her intently, Marcus shook his head. "I'm not sure you do get my meaning. I care about you, Melanie. In a way no boss should feel about an employee."

Even as the husky timbre of his voice bumped up her pulse rate, annoyance stirred inside her. He knew how rattled she still was over Carlos Suarez's sudden appearance. What woman wouldn't welcome an offer to lean on some gorgeous Spaniard for comfort?

But the man gazing down at her was offering much more than just a sturdy shoulder to lean on. What she saw in his dark eyes went way beyond concern. Lust was more like it. That unbridled, scorch-your-skin-off passion reserved for lovers.

"I do get your meaning, Marcus," she said, forcing

a calmness into her voice she was far from feeling. "You want to be more than just my boss at the moment. You're a man, offering comfort."

He rested a hip against the railing. "You make it sound like that's a bad thing." His eyes had darkened, but his tone remained mild. Only a well-honed ear could have detected the steel in it.

"Not totally. I appreciate you loaning me your cell phone. And making sure I was out of earshot of all the stable workers before I dialed 911."

"But?"

"I told you about my past. How a man I cared about— deeply—kept things hidden from me. Lied to me."

Marcus gave her a curt nod. "That cop was married with a baby on the way. I don't have a wife, Melanie. Pregnant or otherwise."

In reflex, her fingers tightened on the railing. She would never forget the day the hugely pregnant redhead confronted her in a mall parking lot. Learning the mortifying truth about the man she loved had hurt more than Melanie had ever hurt before. And she'd be damned if she ever again trusted so blindly.

"So, you're single," she said. "Half-Spanish, half…" She lifted a shoulder. "That's a blank I can't fill in, Marcus. Because you choose to guard every ounce of information about yourself as if it were the Holy Grail. That's your right, but I don't—"

"English. My father was English."

The way his voice had gone so abruptly quiet made her throat burn. "Why didn't you just tell me that the other day in your office when I asked?"

"Dammit, because I don't *feel* half-English." Turning, he swept his gaze over the big house across the drive. "This will probably be hard for you to understand, but I don't have ties to a place like you do to Quest. That's one reason I don't talk about my past. When you left your home, your family, you hurt. When I left, all I felt was relief. And that's what I've felt every time I've moved from one job to another."

He hesitated only a moment, then repeated. "*Every* time."

"What about your family?"

"I don't have one."

Melanie's heart tightened. She couldn't even begin to imagine what it would be like to lose the solid foundation of family she'd always depended on. "No one at all?"

"No." He turned his head, met her gaze. "I meant what I said when I told you that part of me is horse trainer. I train Thoroughbreds. *That* is what defines me. Are you happy now that I've told you these things?"

She might have been if his tone didn't sound as though he'd shoved the words between clenched teeth. Studying him, she saw that his jaw looked ready to crack.

A deep, intuitive disquiet swept through her. There was more, she thought, while the silence that had settled between them seemed to add weight to the cool air. It wasn't just her instincts clanging like a fire alarm telling her that. She saw the truth shadowed in the black-as-night eyes staring into hers.

Melanie felt the sparks kindle between them, the memory of their kiss flaring to mind.

All of which served as a reminder. Although tempting, getting further involved with Marcus Vasquez would not be good for her. Best to think of him as the equivalent of being offered cake and ice cream half an hour before she was due to weigh in for a race.

Totally tempting, but with major consequences attached.

Abruptly she turned, moved to the center of the balcony.

The whine of a saw streamed from the French doors that opened off the big house's flagstone patio.

When the saw fell quiet, she said, "I appreciate you telling me those things about yourself."

"I don't want your appreciation, Melanie."

Her voice softened. "I'm aware of that." And therein lay the problem. She knew exactly what he wanted. She desperately wanted it, too. Just as everything inside her sent the message that jumping into an affair with this man would be a huge mistake.

She shifted to face him. The expression in his eyes made her feel hot and breathless and a little alarmed. Not in fear of him, but of an attraction beyond anything she'd ever experienced.

Lord, she needed to get away from him. "I care about you, too, Marcus."

His brows drew together. "I might greet that news with more enthusiasm if you didn't sound so miserable just saying it."

"I'm sorry, I…" *Don't risk your heart again,* she cautioned. "All things considered, it would be best if we continue on a boss-employee basis."

The churn of an engine had her glancing over her shoulder in time to see a black-and-white police car appear at the top of the driveway.

"I know you have work to get back to," she said while gesturing to make sure the driver spotted her. "I can deal with the police on my own."

"You could." Marcus's boot heels sounded a hard echo against the flooring as he closed the space between them. When he halted only inches from her, Melanie felt as if all the air had been sucked away from the balcony. "But you aren't going to handle them on your own."

His voice was low and as unrelenting as quartz, and had her fighting not to take a reflexive step back. And even though his gaze had darkened with an anger she'd never seen before, she lifted her chin.

"Aren't I?"

"No. Carl Suarez made contact with you on my property," Marcus reminded her levelly. "You work for me. *I'm your boss.* That makes what happened to you this morning my business. So plan on me sitting in on your interview." He swept his right hand sideways. "We'll use your apartment."

Without waiting for her to reply, he turned, strode toward the end of the balcony and descended the stairs two at a time.

It wasn't until he reached the car and shook the uniformed cop's hand that Melanie managed to force the breath out of her lungs. And then drag in another.

"He doesn't take getting dismissed well," she murmured while both men started up the stairs.

For the first time since she'd come to Lucas Racing,

she felt trapped. If she canceled her contract, Marcus would schedule a different jockey to race Something To Talk About. She would lose the opportunity to use her skills to help her financially strapped family.

Lovely, Melanie thought morosely. Her only option was to stay at Lucas and work for a man whom she was afraid—very afraid—she was in danger of falling in love with.

A man she had no idea if she could trust.

IN THE MONTHS HE'D LIVED in Kentucky, Marcus had come to know the roads as well as he knew those on Spain's Costa del Sol. The highways and curving back roads leading to Quest, and now to Lucas Racing, had become a part of his life, and what some people would say led to a feeling of home.

Home, he thought as he steered his sleek silver Jaguar through the gray evening dusk. That sensation was new to him and it had him frowning. Home meant putting down roots. He'd known when he agreed to partner with Demetri Lucas that he would no longer have the freedom to pick up and walk away without a backward glance the way he had from every other job he'd held.

Except for one.

His decision to leave Quest had involved a major emotional struggle. He'd known that paying his hefty salary had become a burden for the cash-strapped Prestons. And that Robbie Preston was more than capable of stepping into the head trainer position. Still, Marcus had felt a wrenching regret over walking away from a woman who had haunted his thoughts since the first time he'd laid eyes on her.

Which had been a major surprise, seeing as how he hadn't intended on getting serious about any woman, much less some curvy little jockey.

Just the thought of his last encounter with Melanie had him tightening his grip on the steering wheel. Forty-eight hours had passed since they stood on the balcony outside their apartments, waiting for the police to arrive. Two days since he told her he had an Englishman's blood flowing through his veins.

And though he had promised his dying mother never to reveal that about himself, there'd been no way he could have continued to keep that part of the truth from Melanie. Not when he'd been so totally, so exclusively aware of her. The way her long, honey-colored lashes framed her blue eyes. The subtle trace of bronze she'd smudged on the lids. The pale moist gloss on her lips.

"Dammit," he muttered. Maybe he should have totally broken the pledge he'd made to his mother. *Maybe* Melanie wouldn't walk away if she knew about his past. Problem was, he didn't know for sure. Couldn't trust that not to happen. So he had no choice but to remain silent in order to keep her close.

Despite the dread now fisted in his chest, Marcus felt a sense of welcome when he steered the Jag between the stone pillars at Lucas Racing. And a completely unexpected flash of pleasure when he saw Melanie's turquoise T-Bird parked in its usual spot.

It was idiotic that a small part of him felt as if he were coming home to her. That she was waiting for him.

As he climbed out of his Jaguar into the slate-blue twilight, he noticed the vehicle parked on the other side of hers. He recognized the red SUV as belonging to her brother, Brent.

Melanie was all about family. At this stage in his life, Marcus knew it was senseless to let himself feel cheated over the hand fate had dealt him. But he couldn't help it. His mother had been kind to him, but deep in his heart he'd known she viewed him as a constant reminder of the man who hadn't wanted her.

He looked up at Melanie's apartment, where shimmery lights glowed and flickered behind the drawn curtains. She had the Christmas tree lit. Candles burning.

Was it so much to wish those lights burned for him?

He curled his hands into fists. A mother's deep, enduring love hadn't been all he'd been cheated out of. He'd finally found a woman he cared about, a woman he *wanted* on more than just a physical level, but a deathbed promise stopped him from going after her.

He had been well aware of the bitter resentment his mother harbored in her heart. In retrospect, he knew he'd been wrong to agree to what she'd asked. But she'd been in the throes of agonizing pain, gasping for air, the hand that gripped his trembling with the hatred he saw in her eyes as she begged him to give her his word.

So, he had.

And now he was paying the price.

Jaw tight, Marcus focused on the lighted window of Melanie's apartment while regret filled the air around him like invisible smoke.

HER APARTMENT COZY with candlelight, Melanie handed her brother a mug of steaming coffee. She settled with her own mug at the opposite end of the couch from him.

"Dinner was great," Brent said, then arched a brow. "Did you learn to cook, or something?"

"Get real. The woman who prepares meals for the stable hands took pity on me when I told her my brother called at the last minute to say he was dropping by." Melanie blew across the coffee's steaming surface before taking a sip. "As you now know, her *lasagna classico* is killer."

"I'll say." Brent retrieved the copy of the trade newspaper off the coffee table. "I bet the observer who snapped this shot of you falling off Something To Talk About got big bucks for it."

"No doubt. The sportswriter filled up three columns with speculation about whether I'll stay in the saddle during the Gulf Classic." Melanie furrowed her brow against the uneasiness that had lain heavy in her stomach since she first saw the article. "I just wish the paper hadn't also run that picture of me talking to Carl Suarez and identified him as the 'frantic son of a murder victim.' I have no idea how the observer who took the photo knew who Carl was."

"I can guess," Brent said. "He's the spitting image of his father. Santos worked around stables all his life. Every observer would know him by sight. When they saw Carl with you, it would have been obvious he was upset. Maybe they wanted to know why and started running some checks. The police report on Santos's murder probably popped up."

"I imagine you're right," Melanie said. To help ward off the evening gloom, she had lit a dozen candles and plugged in the Christmas tree's twinkle lights. But it wasn't just the chill of the evening that sent a shiver up her spine. It was the thought that the teenager who'd witnessed his father's murder was still out there somewhere, scared and alone.

Brent nodded. "I've talked a couple of times to the homicide detective who's working Santos Suarez's murder. As of this afternoon, they haven't found any sign of Carl."

"What about the phone he had that his dad gave him right after the crash? Or my cell? Have they been able to track either one?"

"He made a call on your cell to a pay phone in Mexico. Your phone's been turned off since then." Brent shoved a hand through his dark hair, leaving it rumpled. "He hasn't made any calls on the other phone, which seems to confirm what he said about smashing it against a rock when he fell."

"What about his aunt in Mexico?"

"She swears he hasn't called. And that he hasn't shown up there."

Melanie huffed out a frustrated breath. "The killer wore a ski mask, so Carl didn't see his face. But he did spot the tattoo on the inside of the guy's wrist. Can the police track him that way?"

"They haven't had any luck so far. I went by the Angelina Stud Farm this morning and talked to the employees there. No one remembers having ever seen a guy with a small rectangle half red, half gold tattooed on the inside of his wrist."

"If only Santos had told you the truth about what went on when Apollo's Ice was at the stud farm, he might still be alive." A sense of futility began to rise in Melanie, and with it, anger. "His son wouldn't be on the run from the killer. Our family wouldn't be in danger of losing Quest."

"I've found myself saying a lot of 'if onlys' over the past months," Brent said.

He stared at the newspaper for a few moments, then tossed it back on the coffee table. "Mel, I don't think the killer's a local guy. There's no way to prove this, but there's a chance he also murdered Rory McLoughlin."

Melanie searched her memory for that name. When she found it, her eyes went wide. "The vet who worked at Angelina while Apollo's Ice was there?"

"One and the same."

"Didn't you tell me he was killed in Ireland last month during a botched robbery?"

"It *looked* like a robbery because his wallet and watch were stolen. They could have been taken just to make the death appear to be a robbery gone bad."

"What makes you think both murders are connected? Was the same gun used?"

"I doubt it. Even if the killer is a pro, it would be too hard logistically to smuggle the same gun in and out of different countries. But carrying a gun is like anything else—you find a favorite type and stick with it. A .22 automatic was used to kill McLoughlin and Suarez."

"That could be just a coincidence, right?"

"True. But the ammo used to kill both men ups the odds that the murders are related."

"How?"

"It was subsonic. Meaning, when it's fired, the bullet doesn't travel fast enough to break the sound barrier. Bottom line, it's very quiet."

"So the shot would be less likely to attract the attention of anyone nearby?" Melanie asked.

"Exactly. Which cuts down on potential witnesses." Brent raised a shoulder. "The dead men worked together at Angelina. What's the likelihood they were killed on different continents by assailants who just happened to pick up a box of subsonic ammo?"

Dread crawled over Melanie's scalp. "Did you tell all that to the detective investigating Santos's murder?"

"Yes. He's advised the Irish cops the murders might be connected. They're checking to see if anyone spotted a man with a rectangular tattoo on his wrist around the place where McLoughlin was killed."

"Lord," Melanie said, while a shudder of fear crept up her spine. "Brent, be careful. You've been digging into this since the moment we found out that Apollo's Ice didn't sire Leopold's Legacy. We know now that whoever is behind the fraud is willing to kill to keep people quiet."

"I've got two girls to raise, so you bet I'm being careful," Brent said quietly. "But I'm Quest's head breeder, and whatever happened went on during my watch." A glint of determination settled in his blue eyes. "I'm going to find out who's behind this, Mel. They're going to pay dearly for what they've done to our family."

Melanie couldn't deny that she desperately wanted that, too. "Just be careful, okay?" She forced a smile. "Family gatherings would be really dull if you weren't around to harass me."

"I'll do my best." Brent swallowed the remainder of his coffee. "Speaking of family gatherings, are you still planning on making it to Dad's birthday party?"

"Nothing could keep me away."

"And Marcus? He got an invitation, too."

"He hasn't said," she answered. In truth, he'd said very little to her since their session on the balcony. "Since the birthday party's only two days before Christmas, I'm planning to stay over at Quest."

"It'll be good to have you home for a while."

The sound of heavy footsteps coming along the balcony had Melanie glancing toward the front door. She ignored, *tried to ignore,* the quick frisson that came with knowing Marcus had returned from meeting a potential client.

Knowing he would have seen Brent's SUV parked by hers, she held her breath, wondering if he would stop and knock. Seconds later, she heard the door to his apartment open, then close.

Inside her belly something twisted. Disappointment, she realized. That she had truly hoped he would stop by when she'd made it clear she wanted only a business relationship with him had her giving herself a mental kick.

She couldn't have it both ways. Just because some sort of invisible attraction simmered between them didn't mean she could trust the man with her heart. Not when everything inside her told her to beware.

And how fair was that when just looking at Marcus Vasquez made her think of hot, sweaty skin and tangled sheets?

God, she had it bad.

"Mel?"

Heat flooded into her cheeks when she realized Brent was watching her, obviously waiting for her to reply to something her lust-filled thoughts had blanked out.

"Sorry, what did you say?"

"I asked if you've had time to buy any of the stuff on Katie's and Rhea's Christmas lists." He rose, pulled his car keys out of the pocket of his khaki pants. "They keep searching under the tree for presents with their names on them. There aren't any from me yet."

"There will be soon."

She rose off the couch, slipped on her shoes and carried the coffee mugs to the kitchen. "Tomorrow's my day off, so I'm driving into Louisville to shop."

She retrieved her quilted jacket off one of the long-legged stools at the kitchen counter, tugged it on, then pulled a small paring knife out of a drawer. "I'll bring all the loot over in the next couple of days."

Brent gave the knife a considering look. "Do you think I need an armed escort to make it safely to my SUV?"

"Hardly." Melanie snagged a pear out of the big wooden bowl she kept stocked with fruit on the counter. "Something To Talk About still gets his pear each night after evening stables."

Brent wrapped an arm around her shoulder and

squeezed. "Did I mention I heard the twins say they hope you'll wrap all their presents this year? They think their aunt is the best gift wrapper in the entire world."

"You are so full of it." Melanie used her elbow to give him a jab in the ribs, then skittered from his hold. "How I wound up with such a pitiful brother, I'll never know."

Brent grinned. "You're gorgeous, Mel. Have I ever told you that?"

"Yeah, right." She gave a husky roll of laughter and, hips swaying, strutted out the door ahead of him.

MARCUS STOOD STARING into his refrigerator when he heard the door to Melanie's apartment open. Then he heard her laugh, a rippling, smoky sound that flowed across his skin.

"Jesus," he muttered as the need tethered tight inside him strained hard at that throaty laugh. He knew he was a goner when just a woman's voice had him going hard.

He should stay away from her, he told himself as he closed the refrigerator door with more force than necessary. God knew he should stay away from her. And he figured he had as much chance of doing so as a riding hack had of winning the Triple Crown.

Having lost his appetite, he was debating whether to pull on his coat, go outside and pretend he was there to talk to Brent, when his phone rang.

Marcus checked the number, saw the call was from the owner of the gelding he was currently training. Glad for the reprieve from his own thoughts, he answered the call.

WHEN BRENT'S SUV DISAPPEARED up the drive, Melanie gave the lighted window in Marcus's apartment a final wishful look before she turned and headed toward the stables. With Something To Talk About's pear gripped in her palm, she told herself she was an idiot to have wasted time hoping Marcus would come out, if for nothing else than to say hello to her brother.

How pitiful was that?

Marcus was giving her the space she'd insisted she wanted. At least that's what she *should* want from a man she was so unsure of.

She hated this, she decided as she walked through the spiky shadows thrown by the leafless maples lining the drive. Hated that her body told her one thing, her mind another. Her heart wavered between the two.

Her breath a cloud on the cool December air, she slid open the stable door, feeling each individual pulse point in her body throb in frustration. Not even the familiar scents of horseflesh and fresh hay could take the edge off her nerves.

She was going to have to figure out what she wanted to do about Marcus Vasquez. Soon.

It was late enough that all the stalls had been mucked, their inhabitants watered and fed. By now, most of the hands and grooms would be eating in the communal dining hall, or already retired to their quarters.

Melanie headed down the long corridor lined with stalls. A horse's soft nicker reached her ears.

When she turned in the direction of Something To Talk About's stall, she caught a whiff of scent that had her frowning. *A man's cologne.*

She barely saw the flash of movement, had no time to react before a hand clamped over her mouth. Before she could think to struggle, she was yanked back against a hard body.

The pear went flying.

Panic screamed through her, making everything around her go dim for a moment. She heard her own muffled shout and knew the sound wouldn't carry. She clawed at the hand over her mouth, kicking and squirming in an effort to escape.

When she felt the prick of a knife against the pulse in her throat, she went silent, and deathly still.

"Don't struggle, Melanie." The voice was a harsh whisper at her ear. "Be very still, very quiet, and I won't have to hurt you."

Obediently she let her arms fall limply to her sides. Her heart banged against her ribs like a moth against a screen while her mind raced. She had slipped the paring knife into the pocket of her jacket when she walked Brent down the stairs. Still, she didn't dare go for it while the tip of another knife pressed against her throat.

"Much better." His voice was thickly accented and utterly flat, more frightening than the hiss of a snake. The pressure against her mouth eased slightly. "If you scream, you will die. I don't think you want that."

Tears shimmered in her eyes as she shook her head.

"Good. Now tell me where the kid is."

For an instant, her frantic mind went blank. "What kid?" The terror that bubbled up her throat sounded in her voice.

"Carl Suarez." The man's fingers tightened on her jaw like a vise. "Where the hell did he go?"

Fear skittered up the length of her spine. He might use the knife on her, even if she told him the truth.

"I…don't know…where he went. He…wouldn't tell me."

Melanie winced when the tip of the knife dug into her flesh.

"Do not lie to me! He came to you for help. You gave him money, your watch, your phone. He would have told you where he was going."

She wasn't certain what she would have done—gone for her knife, tried to make the bastard believe her, begged him not to hurt her. But at that moment, a sound echoed at the far end of the stables. A door sliding open?

Her assailant must have wondered the same thing, because he whipped them around toward the sound.

Just as Melanie dragged in a breath to scream, something slammed into the side of her head. A black void opened up beneath her, as if she'd walked off the rim of a canyon in the dead of night.

There was nothing but darkness under her feet.

Chapter Eight

A moan rose in Melanie's throat while consciousness slowly and fuzzily returned.

With a headache raging like twin firestorms in her temples, she chose to keep her eyes closed. Nausea swirled in her stomach. One side of her neck felt as if an ice pick had stabbed into it.

What the hell had happened?

For a moment, she had no clue. The small, vicious explosions blasting in her brain made it too hard to align her thoughts. All she could remember was standing in the drive, watching the rear lights of Brent's SUV disappear into the gloom.

What had she done after that? Where had she gone?

The stables, she remembered with effort. She had

gone to give Something To Talk About his nightly pear. Then the man grabbed her....

Oh, God! The nausea lurched into her throat with the memory of the hard palm that clamped against her mouth, the bite of a knife in her flesh.

With a groan, she lifted a hand to the side of her head and discovered the knot that had formed there. She had no idea what he'd hit her with. But she was still alive, she thought hazily. It was time to figure out where she was.

Dragging in a deep breath, then another, she forced her eyes open.

And felt her blood go cold.

She was lying on her back, on straw in a dimly lit stall with a black-as-pitch horse glaring down at her from six feet above. *Not just any horse,* Melanie realized when she took in the lightning bolt down the center of its forehead.

Who's Cheatin' Who?, the filly with aggression issues. *One hell of a mean horse.*

Ears back and dark eyes looking murderous, the animal wasn't happy to be sharing her stall.

"I'll just get out of your way," Melanie said softly.

The filly reared her head up and swung her body around with startling speed.

Melanie rolled across the hay, barely avoiding the thrashing hooves. The sudden movement increased the pounding in her head. She gritted her teeth against a fresh wave of nausea.

Get sick later, she told herself. *After you get the hell out of this stall.*

When she tried to push herself up, a whirling dizziness set the walls tilting, the gray concrete panels seeming to want to lean in and fall on her. She tried again more slowly and made it to one elbow. Then a knee.

She finally managed to stand, her spine supported against the wall. It took a few moments and several deep breaths before her brain settled into equilibrium.

Careful not to make any sudden moves, she slid her gaze sideways. Her hope of easing around the stall's perimeter, then scrambling over the half door died when she saw that both the lower and upper portions were closed.

The horse whinnied and pawed the ground.

"It's okay," Melanie said, keeping her voice quiet, her tone soothing. "You'll be rid of me in just a minute."

Who's Cheatin' Who? bucked, smashing a steel-clad hoof against the wall.

Melanie's throat went dry. She remembered Marcus saying that the filly's owner had compared the animal to a volcano waiting to erupt. Melanie was very afraid she now stood in the volcano's crater.

Maybe the horse didn't like her talking, she thought. If so, that made it too dangerous to call out for help. But she couldn't just stand in the stall all night, so she had to get herself out. Realizing her hands were gripped into tight fists, she forced her fingers to uncurl. Flexed them.

All she had to do was ease her way to the door, she told herself. One slow, calm step at a time.

Keeping her gaze locked on the filly's liquid black eyes, Melanie took a sideways step.

The horse whinnied and swung its head around,

stamping restlessly from one side of the stall to the other.

Melanie had worked with numerous bad-tempered horses. Some needed cajoling, others a firmer hand. Her method with all of them was to make a gradual approach, slide her fingers beneath the head collar and hold the animal steady while she talked to it. But Who's Cheatin' Who? seemed in the throes of some demonic fit. Her eyes were stretched wide, white showing all round, and she stared as if blind, glaring wildly at nothing at all.

The black nostrils looked huge. As Melanie watched, the horse drew her lips back from her teeth. The ears had gone even flatter against the head and froth formed at the corners of her mouth. It was a face, Melanie thought incredulously, not of unrest or alarm…but of madness.

Holy hell!

The filly backed suddenly away, crashing her hindquarters into the rear wall. Without pausing, she rocked again forward, this time advancing with both forelegs off the ground.

Melanie swallowed a shriek, her breath strangling in her throat as she watched the silvery streaks of thrashing hooves gleam in the stall's dim light. She ducked, pressing her body into the nearest corner seconds before the lethal hooves hit the wall with sickening intent.

Without even taking a breath, the horse whipped around, stood on her forelegs and let fly backward with an almighty double kick that thudded into the panel six inches from Melanie's head. A chunk of concrete splintered off the wall, hitting her right cheek. The stinging pain was followed by a warm trickle of blood.

It was at that moment she began to fear that the bucking, whinnying nightmare might kill her.

With no choice left, Melanie lunged for the door. Her fingers had just wrapped around the handle when the door swung open from the outside with a ripping force.

"What the hell?"

She nearly wept as she threw herself at Marcus.

He grabbed her arms, literally lifting her off the ground as he used a booted foot to slam the stall's door shut.

"You're hurt." His expression was set in almost savage lines, his eyes so bright they seemed to burn her. "What were you doing in with the filly?"

"I didn't…go in on my own." She closed her eyes for an instant. Her heart was hammering, her lungs heaving. "A man knocked me out. I woke up in there."

"Who?" Marcus tightened his fingers on her arms. *"What man?"*

"I never saw his face." She tried to think over the pounding in her head. "He demanded to know where Carl Suarez had gone."

Inside the stall, the horse continued bucking, its hooves thudding against the floor, the walls.

Melanie curled her trembling fingers into Marcus's shirtsleeves. "She's mean, Marcus, but tonight she's murderous. Something's wrong with her. Terribly wrong."

Melanie was vaguely aware of the sound of running feet. Seconds later, the head groom, Billy Tate, raced into view.

"I was just starting my rounds at the other end of the stables when I heard the horse." The man's face was red, his silver hair mussed. When he got a look at Melanie's face, his eyes widened. "Lord, Melanie, you're hurt." As he spoke, he dug a folded handkerchief out of the back pocket of his jeans. "It's clean," he added.

"Thank you, Billy," Melanie said. Without waiting for her to take it, Marcus grabbed the handkerchief, pressed it gently against her bloody cheek.

His other arm wrapped around her waist. "I need to get you to a doctor," he grated.

"No." She lifted a hand, placed it against his and was surprised to feel a vague tremor in his fingers. "Just give me a minute to catch my breath and I'll be okay." She gestured toward the stall. "It's the filly who needs a doctor."

As if on cue, a shrill whinny pierced the air.

Marcus looked at Billy. "A man attacked Melanie," he said, his voice as cold as steel. "Roust all the stable boys and grooms, and have them search the grounds. While they're doing that, take Melanie to my quarters. Call the police, then the vet. Wait with her while I see to the horse."

"Yes, sir."

"Marcus, be careful." Melanie's emotions were rocking, and she couldn't bear the thought of him going into that stall and facing those lethal hooves. But she knew he had to. "Promise you'll be careful. *Promise.*"

"You don't need to worry about me." His eyes had gone from angry to flat and cold. "But whoever hurt you tonight does. I'm going to make him pay, Melanie. I swear it. He's damn well going to pay."

AN HOUR LATER, police cars and a veterinarian's van clogged the drive at Lucas Racing. Marcus paced his living room, his brisk movements fueled by murderous rage. He knew without a doubt that if he could get his hands on the bastard who'd held a knife at Melanie's throat, he wouldn't hesitate to kill him.

Hands fisted, he glanced toward the couch. Melanie sat on one end, holding an ice pack against her right cheek while she talked with the detective who'd shown up a few minutes ago. Grady Quinn had been summoned after the patrol officer who answered the initial call learned that tonight's assault was linked to the recent murder of Santos Suarez.

"Let me make sure I've got all the facts straight," Quinn said. The sandy-haired homicide detective was tall and lean, dressed in a heavy sweater and slacks. "You didn't get a good look at the man who attacked you?"

"I didn't get *any* kind of look at him," Melanie replied while lowering the ice pack. "He kept me in front of him the entire time."

Watching her press her fingertips tentatively to her battered cheek ignited Marcus's fury all over again. He welcomed that fire in his blood. It was preferable to the blank terror he had felt when he swung open the stall door and she'd lunged into his arms. Or the cold fear that ripped up his spine each time he thought about what could have happened to her tonight at the hands of the man who'd attacked her. And left her unconscious and helpless with the filly that Marcus was almost one hundred percent sure had been drugged.

"He was tall," Melanie added. "Muscular. I caught a whiff of his cologne."

"Can you identify the cologne?" Quinn asked.

"No. Something piney. I'd recognize it if I smelled it again."

Quinn jotted notes on the small pad of paper he held in one palm. "Other than asking you where the young man had gone, did your assailant say anything more about Carl Suarez?"

"No." As if to steady herself, Melanie squeezed her eyes shut for an instant. Her hand went from her bruised cheek to the gauze pad taped to one side of her neck. "He…*insisted* that since I had given Carl money, my watch and cell phone that he would have told me where he was going. When I denied it, he dug the tip of the knife into my neck."

When her voice wavered, it was all Marcus could do to hold himself back from going to her.

"That's when you heard the noise at the far end of the stables," Quinn confirmed quietly.

"Yes. It sounded like a door opening and closing." She shifted on the couch, met Marcus's gaze, her blue eyes tight with strain. In the bright light from a nearby table lamp, the raw scrape and purple bruising on her cheek contrasted vividly with her pale flesh. "Was that you I heard?"

"Must have been." He struggled to keep his fury banked, his tone even. "I got a phone call here at the same time you walked your brother to his car. The owner of the gelding I'm training asked me to fax an extra copy of our contract. He needed it first thing in the morning, so I went down to my office to send the fax tonight."

"Did you hear anything out of the ordinary when you got there?" Quinn asked.

Marcus swore under his breath. "If I'd heard anything, don't you think I'd have checked it out?"

"Of course." Quinn held up a hand. "I had to ask."

Marcus battled control back into place. The detective was doing his job, he understood that. "It wasn't until after I sent the fax and walked out of my office that I heard the filly. Horses can't scream, but what I heard was damn close to that. I knew something was wrong."

Just then, a knock sounded on the front door. Marcus turned, pulled it open.

Erik Underwood, a trim, tidy man with a fringe of snowy hair and a ruddy outdoor complexion, stepped inside. Clad in a red flannel shirt and jeans, he nodded to Melanie, then to Quinn, after Marcus introduced him as the veterinarian who tended all horses stabled at Lucas Racing.

"What can you tell me about the filly?" Marcus asked.

"Taking into consideration the dilation of her pupils, the foam in the mouth and the behavior you described to me, I have to agree that she's been drugged."

"Any idea with what?" Quinn asked.

"An idea or two, but they'd just be guesses. I won't know for sure what drug was used on her until I send off the blood sample to a private lab. Tox tests could take a couple of weeks. Maybe longer."

"Is there a way to speed up those tests?" Marcus asked.

"Money," Underwood said simply. "If you're willing to pay a high price for fast results, you'll get them."

"I'll pay," Marcus said. "What about the filly? What can we do for her?"

"Watch her, for now. It would be too dangerous for me to give her something when I don't know what drug she was injected with." Underwood checked his watch. "She was acting somewhat calmer when I left her stall, so the drug seems to be wearing off."

Quinn rose off the couch. "Doctor, if you could wait for me at your vehicle, I've got a couple more questions before you leave."

"Sure."

As the vet disappeared out the door, Quinn turned to Melanie. "If you need to reach me, this has all of my numbers," he said, handing her a business card. "Call anytime if you remember more about the man or the attack itself. Or if you hear from Carl Suarez."

Marcus noted the tremor in her hand when she accepted the card from Quinn. "I will."

She slid her tongue over her bottom lip. "He was waiting for me," she said quietly. "He must have known that I go to the stables every evening at about the same time to take Something To Talk About a pear."

"It looks that way," Quinn agreed. "He also must have known which horse to drug. If you hadn't made it out of that stall, it would probably look like you'd gone in there on your own."

"And my death would be ruled an accident," she finished.

Just then, the detective's cell phone rang. While he

took the call, Marcus watched Melanie as she pushed up off the couch. Her movements were slow, purposeful, as if every muscle in her body was as stiff as cardboard.

"I'm going to my apartment." She retrieved her jacket off the arm of the couch. Instead of pulling it on, she gripped it tight against her breasts as she walked toward Marcus.

His shoulders stiffened against the urge to reach out and grip her arm to lend support. But he held back. She looked so pale and fragile, he was afraid she might shatter if he touched her.

"Let me take you to the E.R." He knew the emotion churning inside him had turned his voice raw, but he didn't care. "It won't hurt to have a doctor take a look at you."

Her mouth curved faintly at the corners. "I recall saying the same thing to you when the filly kicked you in the ribs. You wouldn't go, either."

"Dammit, that's different."

"Hardly. I need a hot shower, Marcus. Not a trip to the emergency room."

Conceding defeat, he pulled open the door, his free hand balled helplessly at his side. "I'll check on you after the police leave."

She reached out as if to touch his arm, then let her hand drop. "That's not necessary."

He felt the ache in his jaw that told him his teeth were clamped together. "*I* need to make sure you're all right."

"Mr. Vasquez, I'd like a word with you."

Melanie glanced at Quinn, then back at Marcus. "I'm okay. I'll see you in the morning."

Biting down on his frustration, Marcus stepped aside. He had checked her apartment earlier to make sure her attacker wasn't waiting inside. He waited until Melanie unlocked the door of her apartment, then closed the door behind her. After he heard the dead bolt snick into place, he turned toward Quinn. And discovered the cop was watching him with an expression of studied neutrality.

"Yes?"

"That phone call was from one of our lab guys." Tapping his notepad against his palm, the detective moved across the room to stand near the door. "He's reviewed the tapes off the security cameras located near your stables. The man who attacked Miss Preston doesn't show up in any of the frames."

"Meaning, he spotted the cameras and knew how to avoid them?"

"That's my guess. So far, we haven't found any trace of him or the vehicle he used to get here. I don't think there's a question that this was the man who shot Santos Suarez in cold blood. Brent Preston suspects that same man may have also murdered the veterinarian who was employed at the stud farm with Suarez."

"At the same time Apollo's Ice was there," Marcus said and raised a brow. "Do you agree with Brent's theory, Detective?"

"The evidence is only circumstantial, but I suspect it's likely we're dealing with one killer. And that his goal now is to find Carl Suarez. The question is, why?"

Marcus scrubbed a hand over his jaw. He'd been too preoccupied with Melanie's injuries, and then dealing with the filly, to think about that. "Carl said the man who shot his father wore a ski mask. Carl can't identify him."

"I doubt if the killer knows that the teenager spotted the tattoo on his wrist. So, if the sole witness to the murder can't ID the killer, why does he need to find that witness?"

Marcus shoved a hand through his hair. "Maybe the killer believes Carl has some sort of evidence?"

"About the fraud perpetrated at the stud farm, is my guess," Quinn said. "We know from what Miss Preston said that after their car was run off the road, Santos Suarez shoved his cell phone into his son's hand and told him to call for help. Perhaps whatever evidence Mr. Suarez had in regard to the fraud is on that phone."

"Could be," Marcus said. "The killer would have no way of knowing that Carl fell and smashed the phone against a rock."

Quinn's gaze settled in the direction of Melanie's apartment. "If he thinks Carl Suarez is in touch with Miss Preston, the killer could very well come back here. With so many personnel off for the holidays, the police department is stretched thin. There aren't any officers available to guard Miss Preston."

"You don't need to guard her," Marcus returned. "I'll do that myself."

Quinn nodded slowly. "After seeing the way you looked at her, I thought you might." He stepped to the door, then paused and glanced back at Marcus. "If the man does return, you're to use only what force is necessary to protect yourself and others. Understand?"

Marcus returned the cop's steady stare. "Sure," he

agreed, keeping all emotion out of his voice. "If I catch the bastard, I'll only do what's called for."

THE FULL IMPACT of what she'd been through hit Melanie while she stood beneath the shower's spray. With the hot water sluicing through her hair and down her body, her legs began to shake. Tears stung her eyes.

Her hands were trembling as she toweled off. During the time it took to blow-dry her hair, she struggled to mentally talk her nerves into calming down. She wasn't some wuss. She was a professional jockey, a *winning* jockey.

At various times, she'd been tossed over fences and hedges. Stepped on by horses weighing over a half ton. She had a patchwork of scars; her medical history listed numerous broken bones, torn tendons and ligaments. A concussion now and then. All of which she'd endured without shedding a tear. Granted, what she'd gone through tonight had been far different, but tough was tough, and she ought to be able to deal with the fallout of all sorts of emotions without turning on the waterworks.

Why the hell couldn't she do that now?

Because she'd never had a man's rough hand clamped over her mouth while he gouged a knife into her neck. Heaven help her, she'd been so scared. *Terrified.*

Her fingers gripped the edge of the vanity while she stared at her reflection in the mirror. With her blond hair combed back off her face, her skin looked as pale as death, a vivid contrast to the angry red slash and getting-darker-by-the-minute bruising on her right cheek. Her eyes shone like overly bright glass beads.

If she hadn't been extremely lucky tonight she'd be dead, either a victim of a stabbing, or trampled beneath a drugged horse's deadly hooves.

The man who'd grabbed her was still out there. He could come back. He could come back with his knife and…

No, she cautioned, even as she shivered against the prickling sensation zipping up the back of her neck. She was shaken enough without scaring herself even more with wild images right out of the slasher stories her brothers used to tell during their childhood campouts.

When a tear rolled down her cheek, she dashed it away. Dammit, she was very afraid she was one sob away from a crying fit, and there was nothing she could do to stop it.

Okay, so maybe after a good cry she would fall into a dead sleep, then by morning be able to distance herself emotionally. Get back to thinking like a normal human being instead of a scared, weepy woman.

Good thing her bedroom was right across the hall. Because it felt like the ETA on that crying jag was about a half minute away and the clock was ticking. She wanted to be snuggled under the covers with a box of tissues when the waterworks started.

She hung up her towel, pulled on her heavy velour robe, then opened the door. And instantly froze.

Marcus stood waiting in the hallway, his dark hair rumpled as if he'd raked his fingers through it, one shoulder propped against the wall as he talked on his cell phone. He'd shoved up the sleeves of the black sweater that she wished to hell would do a better job of hiding the muscular contours of his chest and arms.

"Trust me, Brent, I don't plan to let your sister out of my sight," he said, then folded the phone shut. "How are you doing?"

She angled her chin. "When you said you wanted to check on me, I didn't realize you planned to come into my apartment while I took a shower."

"I didn't *plan* it. When you didn't answer my knock on the front door, I used my key."

She gestured toward his phone. "I planned to call Brent in the morning and tell him what happened."

"I saved you the trouble." Marcus clipped his phone onto the waistband of his jeans. "You didn't answer my question. How are you doing?"

"I'm okay." She fisted her hands so he couldn't see how unsteady they were.

He pushed off the wall and stepped over to her. "You don't look okay."

"Well, here's a news flash, Vasquez, I've had a rough couple of hours, so you'll just have to get past how I look. I'll be fine after I've had a good night's sleep."

"Which is exactly what you need, Preston." He raised a hand and touched her undamaged cheek, stroked his fingertips down her jaw. "I've got something I need to say to you first. It might help you sleep better."

Her pulse jumped in response to his touch. "What?"

"I'm not going to let him get another chance at hurting you," Marcus said softly. "So you're going to have to get used to *your boss* being near. Also, I've hired a security company to patrol the grounds. They start in the morning. Starting tonight, I sleep on your couch."

She wanted to tell him no, that she didn't need a protector. But the truth was, she did.

"Thank you," she whispered and blinked furiously, trying to discourage the tears that still threatened to spill over. "Dammit, I hate being scared. And weepy. I can't seem to stop being either."

"You're not alone in the scared category." He cupped his palm against the side of her throat. "When I pulled open the door of that stall and saw you with blood on your face, it scared the hell out of me, too."

She knew she should turn away from his touch but she couldn't make herself do it. His show of tenderness was too soothing. Too welcome. Another tear slid down her cheek.

She wiped it away. "I *never* cry."

"Come here." He tugged her into his arms, stroked a hand over her hair. "I'm glad you're alive, Melanie Preston."

"Me, too." Her voice quavered at the emotions welling up inside her. "God, Marcus."

Covering her face with her hands, she broke.

"Let it out," he murmured. "You'll feel steadier after you get it all out."

She couldn't stop. His arms were strong, his voice understanding. With her face buried against his hard chest, she sobbed out the fear, the terror.

He rested his cheek on her hair, held her lightly. And waited.

"I'm sorry," she said as the tears finally passed. "I got your sweater all wet."

"It will dry."

She would have pulled away, but he continued to hold her. She squeezed her swollen eyes shut. "You wouldn't have had to deal with that if you'd left me alone."

"Guess you showed me," he murmured before easing her back to study her.

"Guess I did."

Their faces inches apart, he looked intensely at her for a moment, then lowered his head and pressed his lips to hers. Softly, as if his intent was more to comfort than arouse.

She slid her hands up, wrapped her arms around his neck and let the sweet sensation wash over her. As her mouth moved beneath his, she ached and trembled, aware of how close she'd come to death, and how very much this man's touch was bringing her senses to life.

His arms tightened around her. He was holding her so closely now that her breasts were flattened against his chest. The heat of his body seeped through the layers of clothing between them, and the scent of him wrapped around her, warm and masculine.

His touch, his kiss unleashed a deep current of emotions inside her. Passion, need, a dangerous excitement.

Even more dangerous because she wanted it. Wanted *him.* Now. Right this minute.

Her hands clenched his shoulders as she deepened the kiss.

Even as his mouth crushed against her soft lips, Marcus told himself to stop. It wasn't going to be easy, not with those hot, sexy little sounds coming from her throat. Not when her short, neat nails were digging into his shoulders.

Not when she was kissing him back, greedily tasting his mouth as if it were a dessert buffet.

But he knew her response wasn't fueled by desire or even lust, simply a delayed reaction to the attack.

It cost him to draw back, to force himself to clamp a lid on the need that had brewed inside him for months.

"I'm going to hate myself in the morning for saying this," he murmured against her temple. "But I don't think this is the right time to take this any further." His fingers were still caught in her hair and he wanted to keep them there, keep her with him.

It took a few seconds for Marcus's voice to penetrate her hazy thoughts. Another second for Melanie to open her eyes.

Then sanity came rushing back and she nearly moaned as she pulled away.

"You're right." Her voice came out in little pants. Her heart was beating too fast. She couldn't quite catch her breath and her legs had turned to jelly. "God, we shouldn't have done that."

"I don't agree," he said, his voice as ragged as hers. He scrubbed a hand over his jaw. "I just think our timing's off a little."

"Way off." She shoved her hands through her hair. "You caught me off guard. At a weak moment."

Marcus said nothing, just lifted a dark brow.

"You're right," she conceded as if she'd read his thoughts. "It wasn't just you. I kissed you, too, I know that." And if *he* hadn't put on the brakes, she wasn't all that sure she could have stopped herself.

Oh, Lord, if she wasn't careful, she'd be involved in

a full-fledged affair with him before she knew it. Hell, before the night was over. But an affair with a man she didn't fully trust was not what she wanted. She had to get herself under control while she still could.

"Thanks for letting me cry on your shoulder."

"You're welcome."

Turning, she opened the door to the linen cabinet, pulled out a blanket and pillow. "For the couch," she said.

Marcus tucked them under one arm. "Tomorrow's your day off. What do you have planned?"

"Shopping." She pulled in a deep breath. "I need to finish my Christmas shopping and I promised Brent I'd go into Louisville and buy Christmas presents for his twins. I need to buy my dad a birthday present, too."

Marcus gave her a curt nod. "I'll go with you."

When she opened her mouth to protest, he added, "The guy who attacked you tonight wants Carl Suarez. You're his only lead to the boy. Detective Quinn thinks it's possible the bastard might come after you again. Which means you can't go anywhere alone until the police find him."

All it took was the memory of the knife against her flesh for Melanie to change her mind.

"All right, we'll go shopping."

"See you in the morning."

She turned, and walked down the short hallway. Once the bedroom door was closed behind her, she leaned against it.

In the morning, she thought and shut her eyes. Maybe by then her blood would have cooled. Her pulse calmed. Maybe by then she would no longer be able to taste the need—his and her own—that was churning in her blood.

Need that even now she wanted desperately to give in to.

Chapter Nine

Melanie's cell phone rang the next morning just as Marcus steered his Jaguar onto the interstate.

He shot her a look. "I wonder which of your relatives it is this time."

"Who knows?"

When she grabbed her purse off the floorboard, her stiff muscles reminded her all over again of last night's attack. Taking a steadying breath, then another against the panic that flickered through her, Melanie dug for her cell phone. She could still feel the attacker's rough hand clamped over her mouth, the knife at her throat.

How long, she wondered, would it take for those terrifying sensations to ease?

She had to take another breath to steady her voice.

"I think Brent called every Preston in the book after you talked to him."

"Sounds like it."

Already this morning she'd gotten calls from her father, her mother, grandfather and her other two brothers. Her mother had sounded frantic. Her father and grandfather gravely concerned. Both brothers had responded in the same way as Brent, with a cold-as-steel promise to tear the SOB who'd hurt her to bits.

Melanie checked the phone's display. "It's my cousin Elizabeth," she said before answering.

"Lands alive, Melanie, are you okay?"

Melanie couldn't help but grin when she heard her cousin's honey-smooth drawl. "I'm fine." She fingered the bruise on her right cheek. "Just a little worse for wear, is all."

"When my momma called this morning and told me about that bastard holdin' a knife on you, then knocking you out and tossing you in a stall with some crazed horse, I was ready to book myself and Demetri home on the next flight out of Athens. He talked me into calling you first."

Melanie rubbed at the ache that settled in her right temple. With her aunt Diane spreading the word, the Australian Prestons had probably already heard all the details about the attack, too.

"Demetri's a smart man. You're a famous country-and-western singer whose latest album just went platinum. Your sold-out tour's about to wrap up. You can't just drop everything and come here."

"Sure I can. And if you don't convince me you're one

hundred percent okay, Demetri and I are going to start packing our bags."

"I'm super," Melanie said, infusing her voice with energy she was far from feeling. "Awesome. In fact, I feel so good I'm on my way into Louisville right now to finish my Christmas shopping. So, you can relax—"

"Are you alone?" Elizabeth asked, her voice turning sharp. "Momma said you weren't supposed to go anywhere by yourself in case that man shows up again. If no one's with you, you need to whip a U in that cute little T-Bird of yours and head back to Lucas Racing."

Melanie sighed. Every relative who'd called that morning had instructed her not to venture anywhere by herself.

"Marcus is with me. Actually, he's driving so I'm with him. Elizabeth, take a deep breath and stop worrying about me. I'm fine."

"You're going shopping with Marcus? *Marcus Vasquez?*"

Melanie narrowed her eyes. Elizabeth was not only her cousin, but her best friend. Over the years, they had spent countless hours talking about men, broken hearts and romance in general. So, Melanie knew exactly where Elizabeth's thoughts had detoured when the concern in her voice changed to intense interest.

"That's right."

"Lord, he is one fine man. Tall, dark and drop-dead delectable. I won't have to worry a lick if you've got Marcus taking care of you."

Behind her sunglasses, Melanie slid a sideways look at the topic of conversation. He wore a crisp white dress shirt, black slacks and a gray wool jacket. Against his olive skin, his rigorously brushed hair looked even blacker. His chin was smoothly shaven, emphasizing his firm jawline.

He looked good, Melanie thought. A totally different kind of good than he'd looked when she padded into her kitchen at dawn and found him there, shirtless and barefoot while sipping the coffee he'd brewed.

The sight of his broad shoulders and chest darkened by sleek black hair had made her throat go dry. Snug jeans riding low on his narrow hips, he'd gazed at her over the rim of his coffee mug, his dark hair rumpled from sleep, his jaw shadowed by a day's growth of beard. It took all of her willpower to reach for her own coffee mug instead of him.

For the rest of her life, Melanie would remember that pulse-pumping moment.

"You still there, cuz?" Elizabeth asked.

"I'm here."

"Listen, Demetri has lit a fire under the contractor and decorator doing the remodeling to the house. He told them both we want everything done so we can move to Lucas Racing right after Christmas."

Melanie arched a brow. Now that she thought about it, there had been double the number of service vehicles parked outside the big house over the past few days. "Can they get the house finished by then?"

"Shoot, considering what we're paying 'em, they should have wrapped up their work a week ago. Demetri and I want to have a little housewarming between Christmas and New Year's. Of course, being

Demetri's partner, Marcus is invited. So, why don't you just plan on bringin' him along with you? For protection, and all."

Melanie rolled her eyes. She could almost hear the matchmaking wheels in Elizabeth's head turning.

"Why don't we talk about that when you're at Quest over Christmas?"

"Sounds good." Elizabeth paused, then added, "Melanie, you will be careful, right? I don't want anything bad to happen to you."

"I'll be careful," she promised.

Thinking about the incredible kisses she and Marcus shared only hours ago had Melanie sliding another look his way. She knew in her heart if he hadn't pulled back, she wouldn't have. They would have wound up making love.

Her fingers tightened on the phone. She couldn't allow herself that type of madness again. Not with a man she was so unsure of.

"Extra careful of everything," she added quietly before ending the call.

"You didn't tell me you planned to buy out the entire mall," Marcus said hours later while leaning against a department store's display case. Since they'd already made three trips to load the trunk of the Jag with overflowing shopping bags, his hands were currently empty.

Melanie held up a gold chain with a blue stone that winked beneath the store's bright lights. "That's what happens when you shop for eight-year-old twins who are all female. Katie and Rhea both love clothes. Shoes. Jewelry and trinkets."

So did a certain female jockey, Marcus thought. He'd always viewed shopping as a necessary evil, but that hadn't stopped him from enjoying Melanie's obvious appreciation of the clothes, shoes, jewelry and trinkets she'd purchased for her nieces.

That's not all he'd enjoyed, Marcus conceded as she handed the necklace to a salesclerk and asked her to ring it up. Her rich chestnut-colored jacket and trousers hugged her snug little body in all the right places. Her short blond hair fell in soft waves, framing her face in a ring of sunlight. Gold hoops glinted in her ears.

Even from a distance, her scent drifted over him like a gentle stroke of hands.

"I've got one more gift to buy," she said while sliding the boxed necklace into her purse. "A sweater."

"My mind may be glazed over after hours of shopping, but I seem to recall that you already bought the twins sweaters."

"This one is for my dad. For his birthday."

"Which is four days away," Marcus said while they made their way through aisles teeming with shoppers.

"Are you going to the party?"

"Yes. And since you've been warned by every relative you have not to go anywhere alone, you can plan on me driving you."

He saw the brief shadow that passed over her eyes, knew she was remembering the reason for those warnings.

"I'm staying at Quest over Christmas, remember? I won't be going back to Lucas Racing after Dad's party."

"I remember." He was surprised to realize he felt a little cheated about the time they'd be apart, but he understood she needed to be with her family. "I'll drive back and get you after Christmas."

"You're going to get tired of hauling me around," she said as they reached the men's department. "One of my brothers can take me back to Lucas."

He knew she would be safe with any of her three brothers. But every protective, primitive instinct in him was working overtime, fueled by the echoes of fear and anger he'd felt after she was attacked. And later, he had lain awake on her couch, knowing nothing that had happened to him before, nothing that could happen to him in the future would be more devastating than losing her.

He wasn't going to entrust her safety to anyone but himself.

"How about I let you know if I get tired of hauling you around?"

"Fine." She paused at a display of sweaters, checked tags for sizes. "Think this one suits him?" she asked after a moment. The sweater she held up was a fisher-man-style cable-knit in soft creamy wool.

"Perfectly," Marcus said. "Is it the right size?"

"Maybe. Mind if I use you as a mannequin?"

"Help yourself."

Her eyes measuring, she pressed the sweater's shoulders against his. Marcus gazed down at her, taking in the bruise that marred her right cheek, the bandage on the side of her throat that peeked above the neckline of her thin sweater. He wanted to do a lot more than protect her. They'd sparked something in each other that was impossible to ignore. Impossible to resist.

At least for him.

"This should fit Dad," she said while refolding the sweater.

"Melanie."

Eyes blue as a Bahamian bay looked up from beneath silky blond lashes. "What?"

"Let me take you to dinner."

"You already bought me lunch."

"A burger and fries at the mall doesn't count."

She shook her head. "Look, Marcus—"

He slid his hands up her arms to her shoulders and pinned her with a long, focused look. "I know a special place. Let me share it with you."

He waited, watching her while the indecision she grappled with showed clearly in her eyes.

After a long moment, she angled her chin. "Is the food any good?"

Relief was like a cool wave through his blood. "After dinner, you'll swear you just ate the best meal of your entire life. Trust me on this."

She lifted a slim blond brow. "I'll just wait and decide that for myself."

SHE SHOULDN'T HAVE said yes to dinner, Melanie lectured herself while the silver Jag sliced through the early-evening traffic like a shark. Spending the day with Marcus had been agony. Not because she didn't want to be with him.

Because she did.

Which made things worse.

Idly, she fingered the bandage on the side of her throat. In the end, it was his offer to *share* something that had made the invitation too tempting to refuse.

When he turned the Jag into a parking lot, she nearly told him she'd changed her mind about dinner. Then the headlights swept across the building, illuminating a dimly lit wooden sign that displayed a tall, slim flamenco dancer in searing red, her long, elegant fingers holding castanets.

"España," Melanie said, reading the name over the front door. She glanced around the parking lot, noting it was jammed like Churchill Downs on Derby Day. "Louisville has a Spanish restaurant?"

"Only one. It's family-owned, known for its extended menu of tapas." Marcus switched off the vehicle's purring engine. "When you competed in races at the Mijas Hipodromo, did you visit a tapas bar?"

"No." Melanie sent him a sardonic smile. "The closest I got to a bar was when a couple of local jockeys showed up outside the weighing room after the last race with a bottle of Manzanilla. That stuff went down smooth."

"It should have. It's the best sherry in the world."

"So those jockeys claimed. Knowing that didn't help get rid of the headache I woke up with the next morning."

He sent her a slow smile that had her throat clicking shut. "I'll try to make tonight more enjoyable for you."

Inside, the restaurant was dimly lit with a pale glow illuminating a small stage. The walls were dark, the tables crowded with customers. At a thick wooden bar on the side wall, patrons loitered on stools and huddled over their drinks.

Despite having what looked like a full house, the noise level was muted. Melanie breathed in the warm air filled with delectable spicy aromas, and felt her mouth start to water.

She looked up at Marcus. "We may have to wait."

"They're expecting us. I called ahead while you were paying for your father's sweater."

A short, compact woman clad in a black shirtwaist dress stepped to the hostess podium. While she gathered up menus, she glanced toward the door. A smile spread across her face when she spotted them.

"There's my handsome man!"

Marcus gave her a smile that made his dark eyes sparkle. "Hello, Isabel."

"Felix told me you called." Reaching up, she cupped his face in her hands and kissed him on both cheeks.

Melanie was immediately lost when the woman broke into full-throttle Spanish that went far beyond what she remembered from high school classes.

"I have my own stables now," Marcus said, answering her in English. "They keep me busy."

"That's no reason for you to stay away." The sternness in the woman's eyes transformed to interest when she shifted her gaze to Melanie. "And who is this young woman you've brought tonight?"

"Isabel Rios, this is Melanie Preston. She's a jockey."

"You look too tiny to ride those big horses," Isabel said as she grasped Melanie's hand. "They don't bounce you off?"

"Sometimes." The woman's welcoming smile had Melanie liking her instantly. "It smells like paradise in here, Mrs. Rios."

"It smells like my kitchen at home, *muchacha bonita*. And you must call me Isabel, just like everybody. Marcus, go take your girl and sit." She gestured toward the rear of the restaurant. "Felix already has your food started. You won't have to wait long. What about drinks?"

Marcus pressed his palm against the small of Melanie's back. Her pulse jumped at that intimate contact. "Sherry to start?"

She gave him a wry look as she held up an index finger. "Only one glass of sherry for me."

"An amontillado," he said to Isabel. "Escuadrilla."

"*Bueno,*" she said, waving them away.

"Did you order our food when you called?" Melanie asked as she sat across from Marcus at a small table in a stone-walled room with an arched ceiling. Wrought-iron wall sconces provided muted lighting, shedding shadows over the only other couple sharing the cozy space.

"No. Felix and Isabel know what I like."

"Which is?"

"Tapas to start. Paella marinara for the entrée."

"I know what paella is. What exactly are tapas?"

"Sure you want a food lesson?"

"I like to know what I'm eating."

"All right. During the Middle Ages, innkeepers began placing slices of bread on top of wineglasses as tapas. *Covers.*" Marcus nodded at the waiter who approached with a tray holding their drinks and appetizers. Once they were served he continued. "Soon, patrons asked for items like mushrooms, olives, pieces of seafood to accompany the bread. A national tradition began."

"Interesting."

"And delicious." He held up his glass, tapped it against hers. "Here's hoping you'll agree."

Melanie sipped the sherry. It was dry and soft and went down like liquid gold. "Now I remember why I drank so much sherry with those Spanish jockeys," she said. "It's wonderful. Dangerous."

"As is your profession."

She nibbled on a piece of crusty bread layered with spicy shrimp and olives. "And yours."

"I'm not often in danger of getting tossed off and trampled by a half-ton horse racing full-out around a track."

"And I don't stand as much chance as you of getting kicked in the ribs."

Marcus's gaze was like dark liquid. "I saw you ride at Mijas Hipodromo."

Melanie's eyes widened. "That was nearly ten years ago. My initiation into international racing." She shook her head, remembering how young and green she'd been. "Did you train one of the horses I rode against?"

He nodded. "El Tenedor del Diablo. The stallion was the first horse I worked with as head trainer at a nearby stable."

"He beat my horse by a length." She leaned back in her chair, her eyes narrowed. "*You* beat me."

"I watched you that day," he said quietly. "It was easy for me to sense the rhythm that flowed between you and your horse. You may not have won that race, but I knew the way you rode was in the star-making class. You were primed to rocket like a Roman candle in the racing world." He sipped his drink. "That's exactly what you did."

She felt her cheeks warm under his gaze. "If you're trying to make me blush, you're doing a good job of it."

"A man enjoys making a beautiful woman blush."

Since all logical thought seemed to have abandoned her, Melanie decided it was good timing when the waiter reappeared with plates of paella marinara. Another waiter served a ruby-red wine that Isabel Rios had sent with her compliments.

"This is wonderful," Melanie said after her first bite. "Awesome," she added before digging in with gusto.

"This paella is my favorite," Marcus said. "My mother cooked and cleaned house for a man who owned a vineyard. She didn't make enough money to afford all the ingredients that went into it. So she made it often for the vineyard owner's family, and brought what was left over home to me."

Melanie's fork stopped halfway to her mouth. His voice was relaxed, casual, as though talking about himself was something he did often.

Since he'd brought up his past, she decided to plunge in. "What about your father?"

"He and my mother never married." Marcus's face remained impassive as he spoke. "It was hard on her because she loved him. And because she had a child out of wedlock."

"I imagine that was difficult for you, too."

He took a thoughtful bite. "We lived in a small town, so everyone, including my classmates, knew of my status. Young children can be cruel to each other."

"I'm sorry, Marcus."

"Don't be. I learned to defend myself both with words and my fists. Those talents have come in handy."

Still, Melanie's heart ached over the pain he must have suffered through no fault of his own. "You told me that when you left home, all you felt was relief. Was that why?"

Marcus sipped his wine, regarding her with intensity. "It's part of it," he finally answered.

What was the rest of it? Melanie wondered.

During the remainder of the meal, they talked about the upcoming race in Florida.

"So, *hijo,* what do you think of the wine?" Isabel asked, giving Marcus's shoulder an affectionate squeeze.

"Seductive," he said without missing a beat. "Spicy, fruity and smoky."

Isabel turned to Melanie. "And you?"

"He took the words right out of my mouth."

"But not the food," Isabel said, beaming at Melanie's plate. "You may be tiny, but you eat like the horses you ride."

Melanie took no offense because the statement was true. "I'm lucky. I have this hummingbird metabolism. Nothing sticks."

"Good, because you must try our special dessert. *Bizcocho borracho.*"

Melanie made a mental dive into her high school

Spanish. "Cake something?" she asked, giving Isabel a tentative look.

"*Sí.* It is soaked in espresso and brandy, layered with sweet custard cheese and chocolate."

"I can't." Melanie held up a hand in surrender. "I have no room left."

"Next time, then." She laid a check on the table.

"Yes, I'll look forward to it."

After accepting the bills Marcus handed her, Isabel gave him another pat on the shoulder. "Your girl is something, *hijo.* You should keep this one."

Silence hummed for a moment after the woman swept away.

"*This one,*" Melanie repeated. She lifted her glass, sipped the wine, which Marcus had described perfectly. "So, Vasquez, it sounds like you've brought a lot of women here to meet Isabel."

"Only you." He brought a hand to her face, skimming back her hair with his fingers, molding her jawline with his palm. "You're the only woman I've wanted to bring here."

Melanie's hand fluttered up to light on his wrist and trembled. Her voice was just as unsteady. "We should go."

"Yes, we should." But he kept his hand on her face, his eyes on hers as he leaned closer, bringing with him his heady masculine scent. "Have you ever been compelled to take a step that you knew was a mistake? You knew, but you couldn't stop yourself?"

A fog drifted over her mind and she shook her head to try to clear it. "I try very hard not to make mistakes." But she already knew she had made one by spending time with him in this cozy, dimly lit grotto where the warm scent of spices hung in the air. It would be easy—*so easy*—to move closer, press her lips to his.

"So do I," he said solemnly. "Problem is, sometimes I can't help it. Can't help wanting something I know I shouldn't have."

His gaze lowered to her mouth. And as it lingered there, she felt his fingers tighten against her jaw.

Something deep inside of her chose to regard that small, almost imperceptible gesture as a warning. She couldn't help but wonder what secrets he still hadn't revealed.

Even as her pulse shimmied, she leaned back, dragged her fingers through her hair. "It's been a long day, Marcus. We really should go."

"All right." He rose, offered her his hand. "I'll take you home."

Chapter Ten

The main house at Quest was crammed with Prestons. And Prestons made noise. Lots of it. Christmas carols played from the sound system. In a room down the long hall, twins Katie and Rhea played computer games with Robbie's two stepsons. Blasts from a space war raging between alien invaders exploded in the air every few seconds.

All the noise, including the sound of raised male voices, carried into the cavernous kitchen. A debate in progress, Melanie mused as she sliced carrots. The participants sounded like her grandfather, father and maybe Andrew. Probably debating about a horse. A safe bet, considering almost every conversation that took place at Quest had something to do with Thoroughbreds, racecourses or both.

This December, though, those conversations weren't focused on the chances certain horses stabled at Quest had of winning upcoming races. Now, all anyone talked about was the DNA discrepancy and the resulting ban that barred any horse majority owned by Quest from racing. And what might be permanently lost because of it.

Dread whispered through Melanie. She glanced around the spacious kitchen, made cozy by the homey touches her mother had added that gave it the feel of a Tuscan *cucina*. The walls were painted terra-cotta, the cabinets sage, and the floors were creamy, weathered tile. Vivid bits of pottery brightened every available space, and the appliances—all state-of-the-art—were tucked into nooks and crannies to maintain the old-world feel.

Every holiday, Melanie thought. She had spent every holiday of her life in this house with her family. The thought that they might lose Quest had tears stinging her eyes.

Squaring her shoulders, she fought them back. No way would she let her parents see the fear that had kept her chest tight for months.

When she was sure she had control of her emotions, she looked across the granite-topped counter where her mother stood, spreading pale satiny frosting on a four-layer Amaretto cake brimming with ground almonds. Her father's favorite. As was the huge brisket currently baking in the oven that filled the air with delectable scents. With the housekeeper and cook off for the holidays, Melanie and her mother had taken charge of the kitchen. Another Preston tradition.

"Mom, how are you and Daddy doing?"

Jenna Preston glanced up from the cake. Still striking in her midfifties, she was two inches taller than her daughter and just as slim, with short auburn hair. She wore black velvet slacks with a soft coral cashmere sweater that made her skin glow.

"We're fine, now that we've seen you in the flesh and know you're okay." She shook her head, her gold-and-coral drop earrings catching the late-afternoon light that streamed through the windows. "I swear, Melanie, when we heard what that man did, then what you endured in that stall with the drugged filly, we were terrified for you."

"I'm okay." Knowing she'd added to her parents' worries put a chink in Melanie's heart. "It shook me up, too. Big-time. But I really am fine." Or, she would be. Eventually.

"Now that you're home with us, I'm beginning to believe that."

Jenna's gold bangle bracelets jingled like chimes as she dipped her knife into the bowl of frosting and went back to work on the cake. "It was a comfort to know that Marcus was there, taking care of you."

Melanie thought about the feel of his hard, muscled body against hers when he held her as she sobbed. His kisses that had turned her into a simmering puddle of need.

While heat crept up the back of her neck, Melanie lifted her gaze upward, wishing she could see through the ceiling into the second-floor study where Marcus and Brent had holed up.

"Marcus has been…very kind. Compassionate."

"I would think so. You watch a man work with horses for long enough, you know exactly what's in his soul. Marcus cares. You don't see that kind of down-to-earth gentleness in every man."

Jenna turned the cake slowly on its round stand, giving it an appraising look. "Although Robbie's doing a commendable job as Quest's head trainer, we lost a good man when Marcus gave his notice. A gorgeous man, too."

The comment surprised a muffled laugh out of Melanie. "Mom!"

Jenna flipped a wrist, sending the bracelets slithering up her arm. "I only have eyes for your father, but I still know a handsome man when I see one. And don't tell me you haven't noticed Marcus's looks."

"Oh, I've noticed."

"I saw the way he looked at you when the two of you arrived today. It was more than just physical, Melanie. The man has feelings for you."

"You could tell that? Just by the way he looked at me?"

"It was plain as day. So was the emotion I saw in your eyes. You care for him."

"I do. I'm just not sure I should." Melanie frowned down at the carrot and went back to slicing. "It's hard to describe why. Although he's started to share a little of himself, I can't shake the sense there's a part of him that he keeps closed off. I don't think he'll ever let me in. My heart tells me to do one thing, my brain another."

"And you're caught between the two."

"Totally." Melanie lifted a shoulder. "I guess time will tell."

"It always does."

Cake frosted, Jenna stepped around the counter to where her daughter stood.

"To answer your question, your father and I are doing fine. We're going to get past this whole mystery about Leopold Legacy's sire. Eventually. We may lose a lot because of the ban." Her mother closed her eyes for an instant. "Quest, included. If that happens, it will be heart-wrenching. But we won't lose each other. That's what matters."

"Mom." Melanie reached for her mother's hands. They were so strong, she thought. Everything about her mother was strong. "Surely it won't come to—"

"So, what can a man weak from hunger find to eat around here?" Hugh Preston's voice boomed as he strolled into the kitchen. Seamus trotted loyally behind his master, toenails ticking against the tile floor, nose raised to scent the air.

Clearing her throat, Melanie gave her mother's hands a squeeze before she turned. As she did every holiday when her grandfather wandered into the kitchen feigning starvation, she gave him a stern look.

"Grandpa, you were eating lunch when Marcus and I got here. It hasn't been all that long ago."

"Several hours." Dressed in black jeans and a thick red sweater, Hugh filled a mug from the convention-sized coffeemaker that gleamed in the late-afternoon sun. "Since then, I've hiked through the stables, where I had a good visit with Leopold's Legacy. Tossed around a football with my grandchildren. And been lasered to death by a multitude of alien space invaders. A man needs to keep up his strength after enduring all that." He patted the Irish wolfhound's shaggy head. "Right, Seamus?"

Hugh got a sloppy doggy grin.

Melanie sent her mother a knowing look. "Grandpa wants the leftover frosting."

Jenna held back a smile as she retrieved the bowl. "What's new?"

"I can't help it if my daughter-in-law makes the best frosting in the world, can I? Since she learned that recipe from my Maggie, I get first claim to what's left over. It's a Preston tradition, after all."

Melanie pulled a spoon out of a drawer, rose on tiptoe and pressed a kiss to his weathered cheek. "Us Prestons gotta keep our traditions intact."

"Amen, Granddaughter."

When the telephone rang, she turned, grabbed it off the counter and answered.

"Melanie is…you?" a young, scared voice asked, fading in and out over the bad connection.

Melanie's heart jumped into her throat. "Carl?" Hoping to get rid of the static, she moved to the far end of the kitchen. "Carl, where are you?"

"This…working."

"What?" Straining to hear, she pressed the phone harder against her ear. "We have a terrible connection."

"Gonna…back."

"Carl, I can barely hear you. If you can hear me, just listen for a minute. The man who killed your father is still looking for you. Wherever you are, you need to go to the police. Get to safety. Then call me. I'll help you. *Please,* Carl."

While she strained to hear the teenager's reply, Melanie looked up. Her mother now stood beside her grandfather, her hand gripping his arm. Both watched her, eyes crimped with concern.

"Carl? Carl, are you there?"

Melanie heard nothing but silence.

MARCUS STOOD BEHIND the massive desk in the second-floor study, gazing down at the stacks of files and spreadsheets Brent Preston had prepared. Across the paneled room that sported three walls of floor-to-ceiling bookcases, flames ate greedily at the dry wood in the enormous gray stone fireplace.

"It's hard to believe this all started with what was thought to be a glitch in the Jockey Association's computer system."

"Yeah." Brent tossed a file folder on the desk. "That 'glitch' turned out to be an employee with an admin ID logging on to the system and changing the DNA profile of certain Thoroughbreds to match Apollo Ice's."

"What was the employee's name?"

"Ross Ingliss. He quit his job a couple of months ago, supposedly to go to Russia to marry an online bride. That turned out to be a lie." Brent gestured toward the stack of file folders. "I picked up Ingliss's trail in New York City, then tracked him to a mansion in Savannah, which he paid cash for. I also uncovered his name on passenger lists of flights to the Cayman Islands."

Marcus slid a hand into the pocket of his slacks. "Let me guess. He didn't go there for the white sandy beaches."

"More like for their shadowy banking practices," Brent added, frustration ripe in his voice. "Dammit, Marcus, this guy is like a ghost. Each time I feel like I'm getting close, he disappears."

"Have you been able to link him to anyone who has a grudge against your family?"

"No, and I looked hard for some kind of tie between him, our past and present employees and business associates. I even checked to see if Ingliss had some sort of connection with any member of the family. All dead ends."

"Do you think Ingliss did this on his own?"

"No. From what I've learned, the guy has tech smarts. But he doesn't know his way around a stable or a stud farm. So there's no way he could mastermind a plot that centers on Thoroughbred DNA. All of my instincts tell me there's someone else calling the shots. Someone who paid Ingliss to falsify the information he inputted into the Jockey Association's computer system."

Nolan Hunter? Marcus wondered. His half brother and owner of Apollo's Ice had grown up in a world with Thoroughbred racing as a backdrop. And as the current Viscount Kestler, he'd inherited not only a title but the money that went along with it. Still, Marcus conceded, a title and wealth didn't make Hunter guilty.

Hands fisted, Brent walked to the small bar, sloshed two fingers of whiskey into a tumbler. "Whoever the mastermind is, he's destroying my family's reputation and heritage, and draining it of its fortune. And it's all happening on my watch."

The anger Marcus heard in Brent's voice shone in his eyes as he offered the glass. "Join me?"

"No, thanks." Marcus looked back at the spreadsheets. "As Quest's head breeder, it's understandable you'd blame yourself. But you aren't responsible for what went on at Angelina Stud Farm."

"Dammit, I was *there* during the breeding. So was Carter Phillips," Brent added, referring to Quest's seasonal vet. "We saw Apollo's Ice cover Leopold's Legacy's dam. That's why it's so hard to believe Legacy's DNA proves he's not related to Apollo's Ice."

"You and Carter weren't with the mare who gave birth to Leopold's Legacy the entire time she was at Angelina. Clearly, something went on behind the scenes."

Brent took a sip of whiskey. "That doesn't mean I sleep any better when I think about what this is doing to my parents. My family."

The brisk crackling of flames in the big stone fireplace was the only sound to break the silence that followed.

"What about the two men who worked at Angelina when Apollo's Ice was there?" Marcus asked after a moment. "Melanie said, because of the ammo used, you think Santos Suarez and the Irish veterinarian were murdered by the same man."

"I'd be willing to bet on it. And that he's the bastard who nearly killed my sister at your place."

Just the reminder of that had Marcus curling his hands into fists. "Everything started when Apollo's Ice arrived at the stud farm five years ago," he said levelly. "I know you flew to London to talk to the stallion's owner."

Brent nodded. "I got the impression Nolan Hunter is as puzzled by everything as we are."

"You're sure about that? About Hunter?"

"As sure as I can be without hooking the viscount up to a polygraph," Brent said.

"Carl Suarez just called."

At the sound of Melanie's voice, Marcus looked toward the doorway. Her face was so pale that the bruise healing on her cheek looked new.

"What did he say?" he asked, stepping around the desk.

"I'm not sure. It was a terrible connection. I could barely hear him." When Melanie paused inches from him, Marcus saw the despair in her eyes. "He said something about working and going back."

"Going back where?" Brent asked.

"I don't know. That's all I got." She stabbed her fingers through her blond hair, leaving it mussed. "I told him that the man who killed his father is still looking for him. That wherever he is, he needs to go to the police. I told him I'll help him. I have no idea if he even heard me."

Marcus settled his hands on her shoulders. "Maybe he'll call back."

"God, I hope so." She looked at Brent. "Is there a way the police can find out where the call came from?"

Brent stabbed a button on the desk phone, checked the display. "Caller ID says 'unavailable.' The police can check to see if Carl made the call from the cell phone you gave him. If so, they can get an approximate location."

Melanie nodded. "Before I came upstairs, I dug Detective Quinn's card out of my purse and called him. I got his voice mail, so I left a message. I asked him to let me know if he finds out anything."

"You've done all you can," Brent said.

The clatter of racing feet sounded in the hall. Seconds later, Katie and Rhea exploded into the room as if fuel propelled.

"Daddy!" the twins said in unison. "Grandma said it's time to come carve the brisket."

"I guess Grandpa's decided to pass that honor on to you," Melanie said while squatting to retie one of her niece's sneakers.

Marcus studied the twins. Their hair had been woven in the same intricate braid. They were dressed in identical Christmas sweaters, corduroy pants and eye-popping yellow sneakers. Although they had spent a lot of time in the stables while he worked at Quest, he had never had any luck telling them apart. It was as if someone had made a carbon copy of a single pretty face with huge, break-your-heart blue eyes.

Brent crossed his arms over his chest and regarded his daughters with a solemn look. "And just what are you two going to be doing while I slave in the kitchen?"

"Grandma said we can put candles on Granddaddy's birthday cake."

"He gets *sixty* candles," the other twin said. She cupped her hands around her mouth and whispered, "I don't think the cake has room for that many."

Brent chuckled as he took each of their hands. "Better not let Granddaddy hear you say that," he said before they stepped into the hallway.

Marcus waited until they were out of earshot to speak. "Melanie, are you okay?"

"I'm fine. It's Carl I'm worried about. He sounded

so scared. So lost. I'm terrified knowing that man who attacked me is still out there, looking for him." She shook her head. "He'll kill Carl if he finds him."

"We just have to hope the kid heard you tell him to go to the cops. And does it."

Just then, her grandfather's voice boomed from downstairs, singing a vibrato rendition of "Frosty the Snowman." The blasting notes were joined by Katie and Rhea's high-pitched giggles.

Melanie glanced toward the door. A smile flickered over her face when she turned back to him. "Don't say I didn't warn you about the noise level when the Preston clan gets together for the holidays."

"So far, my hearing's still intact," Marcus acknowledged as he took in her trim, hunter-green sweater and snug black slacks. Her tousled blond hair framed her face. Subtle hues of smoke and teal turned her eyes an electric blue that all at once seemed to have the power to make his heart race.

He wanted to believe it was because her looks were so compelling, her body sleek and arousing. But he knew it wasn't desire that was working in him now. He understood passion, need, hungers. This was more. This was all encompassing.

Good God, he thought, his throat tightening. Was he falling in love? Not likely, another part of him countered. Not after he'd grown up watching the suffering that came with the emotion. Not after he'd sworn he would run for cover before ever letting himself get caught up in anything close to what his mother had gone through.

Still, his world revolved around off chances and long bets, and he knew that odds got defied all the time.

Why—or how—Melanie Preston had swept across the distance he had learned to establish between him and the women in his life, he didn't know. At this point, it didn't matter. He was teetering on the edge of love. Teetering, yet keeping a huge secret from her because of a deathbed promise to his mother.

And what if he could bring himself to break that promise and tell Melanie? he wondered as he breathed in the scent of her hair, of her soft skin.

No, he decided. Just the thought of her walking away chewed up his insides. Throughout his life, the circumstances of his birth had cheated him out of many things. As a child, he'd been helpless to change that. Now that he'd found the woman he wanted, he was determined not to allow anything from his past to get in his way. So, he would keep his promise to his mother and remain silent.

Maybe, just maybe, this would be another case where the odds got defied. After all, Brent had just confirmed he considered Nolan Hunter blameless in perpetrating the DNA fraud. If his own luck held, Melanie would never have to know he was linked by blood to the owner of the horse that had brought on her family's nightmare.

Without thinking, Marcus lifted his hand and tucked her hair behind her ear. "How about we head downstairs and help celebrate your dad's birthday?"

LATER THAT EVENING, Melanie stepped into the conservatory where the Christmas tree soared to the ceiling, its glossy pine branches heavy with silver ornaments and twinkling lights. An ocean of colorful presents pooled beneath it.

She could hear the hum of conversation and laughter coming from the gathering room where the family had retreated after dinner to devour her father's birthday cake. Since it was late enough that the youngest Prestons had all been sent to bed, the noise level had dropped several decibels.

She turned the dimmer switch to bring the room's lights down and enhance those on the tree. As she stared at the soaring pine, she realized just how much of her life she had always taken for granted. Year after year, expecting things to continue, never changing.

"Melanie?"

Startled, she looked over her shoulder, saw Marcus, tall, sinfully handsome, standing in the center of the doorway. He wore dark slacks and a midnight-blue shirt, and he carried his leather bomber jacket in one hand.

As always, the sight of him had her blood heating.

"I'm going to head back to Lucas Racing," he said. "I wanted to tell you goodbye. And wish you a merry Christmas."

Lord, she didn't want him to go. Didn't want to spend Christmas away from him. But since just looking at him had every self-defense mechanism she possessed all but falling apart, she knew his leaving was for the best.

She needed time and distance to figure out how she felt about him. And what, if anything, she was going to do about those feelings.

"Thank you for giving my father the perfect birthday gift."

He moved farther into the room, his footsteps sounding hollow echoes against the waxed-to-a-sheen hardwood floor. "I thought the history of Thoroughbred racing in Spain might interest him."

"It was a super present."

"I'm glad he liked it. I have a great respect for your father. For your entire family." He glanced around. "The last time I was in this room was for Shane and Audrey's wedding reception. It looks totally different now with the furniture back in place."

"Different, but the same."

"Meaning?"

"I was just standing here thinking that I don't know how my parents do it."

"Do what?"

"Every year, they manage to find the perfect tree. From the first Christmas I remember, there's been a tree in that same corner. And each one has always been the perfect height and shape, with heavy, glossy limbs that we decorate with silver ornaments. *Those* ornaments."

"I suppose Santa used to show up every year, too?"

"Of course. My brothers and I used to sneak down and huddle in a corner of the gathering room because that's where the fireplace is. We'd spend hours watching for Santa to come down the chimney. We always wound up falling asleep so we never *saw* him. But there were presents from him Christmas morning."

"Naturally."

"I was standing here, thinking about all that. About

how I don't have one single bad memory in this house. It's hard to even imagine the possibility that it might not be in my family much longer."

When Marcus settled a hand on her shoulder, she felt her insides tighten. And told herself it was her imagination that she could feel the warmth of his touch through her sweater.

"Even if that happens, you'll carry the good memories with you," he said.

She looked up. His eyes were dark, unreadable, giving no hints about his inner emotions. Since he had talked about his mother the other night at the restaurant, maybe he would be willing to offer another personal glimpse about the woman who'd raised him. And himself.

"Did you and your mother have Christmas traditions?"

"I wouldn't call them traditions." Marcus removed his hand from her shoulder, stepped a few feet away to the hunter-green couch plumped with overstuffed pillows. "I told you my parents never married."

"Yes." She watched him drape his leather jacket over the back of the couch.

"That's because my father was already married. As far as he was concerned, his affair with my mother had run its course. He wanted nothing more to do with a lover who had been careless enough to become pregnant. The last time she saw him was two days before Christmas when he broke things off.

"Every December after that, the memories became too much for my mother. She tried to battle the depression, the sadness, but they were there, touching everything. That's my Christmas tradition."

Melanie curled her fingers into her palms against a rush of sadness and sympathy for the pain that Marcus and his mother must have felt. "Did she talk to you about your father?"

"Only to say he had shunned us both. The entire time I was growing up, she never told me his name."

Melanie blinked. "You didn't even know who he was?"

"No, and I didn't *care*." His gaze shifted to the tree. Melanie could see the emotion in his eyes now, the shadow of old pain.

"It wasn't until I was grown and my mother lay dying that she told me his name," he said after a moment. "She asked me to bring the man she'd never stopped loving to see her one last time. So I went to England and found my father. I told him who I was, and asked him to fly with me to Spain to grant my mother's dying wish. He refused. He wouldn't even bend enough to phone her."

"Oh, Marcus."

He held up a hand. "I'm not telling you this because I want your pity. The man meant as little to me as I did to him. When I returned to Spain alone, I saw the heartbreak in my mother's eyes turn to hate. Only hours before she died, she secured my promise to never tell anyone the name of the man who had humiliated her and scorned me."

He stared at Melanie, his face tense, his eyes cheerless in the dim light. "I've kept that promise to my mother. I must continue to keep it. You understand why I cannot tell you his name?"

There was very little he could have said, and nothing he could have done, that would have gotten through her defenses more thoroughly. Touched and shaken, she nodded. "Yes. Thank you for sharing that with me."

He slid his hand into the pocket of his jacket, pulled out a small, brightly wrapped box. He stepped closer to her, handed her the box.

"Marcus?"

"Since I won't see you on Christmas Day, I wanted to give you this to open now."

Her hands shook as she tore off the paper. When she lifted the lid, her eyes went wide at the sight of the gold chain dripping with colorful crystals.

"I looked at this necklace while we were shopping."

"*Mooned* over it is the correct term," Marcus said as he retrieved it from the box. He stood behind her, fastened the chain around her neck.

"Thank you." Melanie turned to face him, her fingertips stroking the beads. "I don't have anything for you."

Marcus glanced up. "I think your grandfather has taken care of that for you."

Melanie followed his gaze to the sprig of mistletoe hanging in the doorway. She hadn't even noticed it before now. "He used to only hang mistletoe in the stables," she said.

"That just goes to show some traditions change." With his fingertips, Marcus traced the line of her arm, from elbow to shoulder. "Maybe for the better."

Her breathing went shallow, but her voice held steady as his thumb rubbed the side of her throat. "Maybe."

Cupping his hand around the back of her neck, he slowly pulled her to him. "We should honor all traditions," he murmured.

He lowered his head to catch her bottom lip lightly between his teeth. Her breath shuddered out. His familiar taste seemed even more potent, like some dark, slow-acting drug that had already seeped into her blood to addict her.

When his mouth settled on hers, she snaked her arms around his neck, her mouth moving avidly under his. Desire arched through her, hot and exultant.

While his mouth fed on hers, she felt his hard, seeking fingers run up and down the nape of her neck, filling her mind with images of what they could do to her body.

Her knees shook as her fingers locked tight behind his neck. Passion rose inside her like a hot, sultry wind when he took his lips on a long, mesmerizing journey over her face with kisses as hot as a thousand honeyed brands. She heard the thick echo of her heartbeat, then nothing but the whisper of her own name as he traced her ear with his tongue.

A grinding, glorious ache settled deep inside her. Melanie pressed the length of her body against his while searching and finding his roaming mouth with her own.

He groaned like an echo in the night and she felt his desire for her against her belly.

His hand slipped beneath her sweater, his fingertips cool against her heated flesh as they slid up her ribs. Then his hand cupped her breast, protected only by thin black lace. His breath grew jagged when her nipple peaked against his palm.

Melanie fisted her hands in his hair while his touch, his tongue half scrambled her brain. She wanted more. She wanted all.

A rush of need, hard, sharp-edged, had her muscles going from hot wires to soft wax. She gripped his shoulders, holding on tight to the firm body that transmitted both safety and danger.

"Melanie…" He whispered her name as he changed the angle of the kiss. "Come with me…"

Her heart raced. Her breathing quickened as if trying to outrace her heart. Heat and need and want balled inside her with the intensity of an inferno.

She needed him. However much that might terrify her, for now the knowledge and the acceptance flowed through her like wine. She would go with him, she thought hazily. Anywhere.

She pulled back to tell him that. But her pulse throbbed, her lungs heaved, screaming for air, and she had no breath left for words.

Which was just as well because at that moment, she caught movement out of the corner of her eye.

"Boy, we thought we were never gonna get here— Oops!"

Melanie turned toward the doorway in time to see her cousin Elizabeth wince. Behind her, Demetri Lucas grinned.

Even as Melanie plastered on a smile, she heard Marcus's soft curse.

Chapter Eleven

"I love all my Preston relatives," Elizabeth Innis said two hours later as she plopped on the opposite end of the quilt-covered sleigh bed from Melanie. Leaning forward, the award-winning singer handed her cousin a bowl brimming with chocolate raspberry swirl ice cream. "But I thought I was never gonna get away from them so you and I could have a girl-talk session."

They had settled in the upstairs bedroom that had been Melanie's for all her life. Filled with English walnut furniture and softened by pillows and bright fabrics, the room still held the personal items she had left behind when she moved to Lucas Racing.

"We could have put this off until tomorrow," Melanie said. After telling Marcus good-night, she had made a swift exit from the conservatory, bounded up the stairs and changed into boxers and a red tank top that sported Quest's logo. It had taken all of her control not to think about what she would be doing at this very moment if Elizabeth and Demetri hadn't shown up when they did.

She would have left with Marcus. Gone anywhere he wanted. Jumped into bed with him.

Lord, what had she been thinking?

"Are you kidding?" Elizabeth asked as she plumped the pillow she'd wedged behind her. That done, she adjusted the belt of her silky white robe, then settled back with her own bowl of ice cream.

"No way am I going to wait until tomorrow to talk to you about that kiss. I'm surprised there wasn't steam coming up from the wood floor where you and Marcus were standing. Do that again, your daddy's going to have to put asbestos on the walls."

Since she still felt as if she were plugged into a two-twenty-volt line, Melanie made no attempt to correct her cousin.

"Spill it," Elizabeth said. "How long have you and Mr. Gorgeous-Available-Intriguing been involved in a relationship?"

"We don't have a relationship." Melanie jabbed her spoon at her ice cream. "We just kissed."

Elizabeth arched a perfectly plucked blond brow. "Okay, no relationship. How many times have you and Marcus 'just kissed'?"

"A couple." Melanie frowned. "Three."

"Well, let me officially apologize for Demetri and I showing up when we did and interrupting kiss number three. And putting the kibosh on number four…not to mention whatever else might have followed."

Melanie held up a hand. "Don't apologize. I'm thankful you and Demetri walked in. If you hadn't, I'd have left with Marcus. *Slept with him.*"

"So, you're not having a relationship." When Elizabeth flipped her wrist, light glinted off the big-as-a-jelly-bean diamond on her engagement ring. "But you're ready to sleep with him?"

"No. Yes." Melanie shoved her bowl aside. "I don't know what's happening to me, Elizabeth. Since the instant I got involved with Marcus I haven't been able to keep up. When I'm with him, I tell myself I shouldn't be. When we're not together, I wish we were."

"Like right now? You want to be with him, instead of here?"

"Exactly. And that's so not what I should be wanting." She could still feel the imprint of Marcus's mouth, hands, body on hers. Could still taste him. And, heaven help her, all she wanted to do right this instant was to taste him again.

"Why is wanting to be with him such a bad thing?"

"Because I don't know him. Even though he's started opening up and telling me about his past, I don't *know* him."

Shifting, Melanie pounded the pillows banked behind her into submission, then looked back at Elizabeth. Slim with short blond hair, the top-of-the-charts singing sensation had a makeup artist, stylist and masseuse at her beck and call. But sitting there, huddled on the bed in her nightgown, her face freshly washed and her hair brushed back off her face, Elizabeth Innis's natural beauty shone through.

Melanie didn't just love her cousin, she adored her generosity of self, her quiet humor, her unshakable loyalty and her amazing lack of self-awareness.

"Demetri and Marcus haven't been partners for long," Elizabeth said around a bite of ice cream. "So they don't know each other all that well, either. Even so, Demetri trusts him totally. He always says that when Marcus tells him something, he can take it to the bank. And if he makes you a promise, it's as good as gold."

"I feel the same way about Marcus when it comes to our working together," Melanie said. "He's the top Thoroughbred trainer in the country. Maybe the world. But that's not what I feel when it comes to the man-woman thing. I know as well as I know my own name that, no matter what Marcus has told me about himself, he's holding something back."

"And that scares you?"

"It terrifies me."

"Sweetie, are you sure you're not just letting your past with that philandering cop hold you back? Just because there was one bad apple in the barrel doesn't mean all the other apples are rotten, too. Melanie, it's been two years since you told that horndog to go to hell. Love will never come again unless you give it a chance."

"Love?" Just the word put a clutch of panic in Melanie's stomach. "Who said anything about love? What's between Marcus and me is just a simple matter of biology. Hormones. Testosterone. You know what happens when two people get stirred up over each other."

"I do, yes," Elizabeth murmured.

Melanie snagged her bowl, sampled the ice cream. Despite her emotional turmoil, the combination of rich, luxurious chocolate and tangy raspberries had her sighing. She relaxed enough to settle back into the pillows.

After a second bite, she said, "This is what I get for purposely staying celibate for two years." She wagged her empty spoon at Elizabeth. "Then along comes this sexy Spanish hunk and all of this pent-up lust just started oozing out of every pore on my body. It's no wonder I can't think straight when I'm around Marcus."

"Well, if all that's involved is lust on your part, why does it matter if he's keeping things to himself? Like you were so fast to point out, no one mentioned anything about being in love. Maybe you ought to just jump into bed with the sexy Spaniard and work off some of that pent-up lust. Have a good time while you get the man out of your system."

"You're right." Melanie leaned forward slowly. "I'm making this complicated when it's totally simple. If what's between Marcus and me is all physical, it shouldn't matter if he keeps things about himself from me…." Melanie trailed off, undone by Elizabeth's patient gaze. "But it does matter," she acknowledged with a groan. "It totally matters. Holy hell, Elizabeth, have I gone and fallen in love with him?"

"You're the only one who can answer that."

"But that's just it, I don't know." Frustration made Melanie's head pound. "Everything is so balled up inside of me. I need to find my balance, and Marcus just keeps throwing me off."

She slid her fingertips over the crystal beads on the necklace he had given her only hours ago. When she'd changed into her pajamas, it hadn't occurred to her to take it off. *She didn't want to take it off. Ever.*

"So, I guess it's a good thing I won't see Marcus over Christmas. Maybe with a little distance, I'll have a better perspective." She spooned up more ice cream and put some effort into making her lips curve up. "Once I figure things out, I'll go from there."

It was Elizabeth's turn to wag her spoon at Melanie. "There's just one little glitch to your not seeing Marcus over Christmas."

"What glitch?" Melanie glanced at the clock on the nightstand. "Marcus should be back at Lucas Racing by now. He's not planning on coming back to get me until the twenty-sixth."

"Do you remember he and Demetri went off to talk business after we interrupted y'all in the conservatory?"

"Yeah, I seem to recall that."

"Well, one thing Demetri was planning on asking Marcus was if he'll come back here Christmas night for our wedding."

Melanie put her hand to her chest. "I thought you and Demetri were going to wait to get married until next spring when you're between tours."

"That was the plan. But with Demetri retired now from Formula Gold racing, we'll be spending a lot of time together while I'm on tour. He'll be going around to racetracks, looking at more Thoroughbreds to buy for the new stables." Elizabeth set her bowl aside. "You know me, Melanie, I'm an old-fashioned girl at heart. The thought of Demetri and me living in sin all those months bothers me. So, we're gonna get married downstairs on Christmas night. I want you to stand up with me."

"You know I will." Grinning, Melanie reached out, took her cousin's hand. "You must have a million things to take care of. Why didn't you tell me about the wedding the other day when you called? I could have helped you with everything that probably needs to be done."

"I hired a wedding consultant, and she's dealing with everything. I didn't tell you because when you and I talked the other day, we were both on cell phones. Reporters know all sorts of ways to eavesdrop on conversations. I can't sneeze without the media knowing about it. Neither can Demetri. We want our wedding to be just a family affair and I didn't want to chance someone overhearing us. The only people we told before now are my mom, yours and Demetri's father. We swore 'em all to secrecy."

Melanie angled her chin. "Now I know the real reason Demetri lit a fire under the people working on the house at Lucas Racing."

"That's right. We'll be moving in right after our honeymoon. And since you work at Lucas, we'll get to see each other all the time. We want you to live in the big house with us."

Melanie opened her mouth to accept the offer, then closed it when it hit her that she would no longer be in the quarters next to Marcus's. She had gotten used to hearing his footsteps, felt a sense of comfort in knowing he was close by.

"Why don't we both think about that?" she said.

"You and Demetri will be newlyweds. The last thing you need is company."

"You're family, not company," Elizabeth said. "But if you'd be more comfortable living where you do now, that's fine, too. You just let me know what you decide."

"Deal."

Sighing, Elizabeth beamed a smile. "Remember when we were growing up how we used to spend hours talking about what kind of wedding we wanted? I'm gonna live my dream. I've got a beaded satin dress that's the most beautiful thing I've ever seen. Luscious flowers, melt-in-your mouth cake and enough champagne to fill the swimming pool. The whole shebang. My momma's flying in tomorrow. So is Demetri's father."

Melanie grinned. "You forgot to mention that the man of your dreams will be there, too."

"Oh, yeah, *him,*" Elizabeth said and laughed. "Sometimes I still can't believe I found Demetri. It feels like such a dream, I have to pinch myself."

Melanie chuckled. "It's no dream, cuz. And it sounds like you've got everything covered."

"I sure do." Elizabeth's smile turned smug. "Just wait until you see the bridesmaid gown I had designed for you. It's gorgeous. Sexy. When Marcus sees you in it, his eyes'll pop out of his head and land on his shoes."

"That'll be something," Melanie murmured.

Marcus, she thought. Was she truly in love with him? If so, what was she going to do about it?

ON CHRISTMAS EVENING, Marcus stepped into the conservatory at Quest, which was lavishly bedecked with satin bows and flowers in what one of the twins—Rhea, or had it been Katie?—had moments before enthusiastically informed him were Elizabeth's colors of silver and pale blue. The white lights on the soaring tree and candles in dozens of candelabra placed around the room provided the only illumination.

Since the wedding was about to begin, he kept well to the back of the family members already seated in the chairs that had been set up to give the conservatory the feel of a small chapel. Soft music played from the stereo system. He heard a few murmured comments and sighs when the music changed to a violin rendition of the "Wedding March."

He turned, saw Melanie start down the long white runner that formed an aisle between the chairs.

Her pale gold hair framed her face in soft curls. As she walked, light winked off the shimmery fabric of her slim, close-fitting silver gown. She carried flowers in her hands; more were scattered in her hair. Cascades of glittering gems swung at her ears. When she passed him, her blue eyes as soft and dreamy as the music, he felt a longing so deep, so intense, he could barely keep from speaking her name.

And he knew, in that one heartbeat of time, that he'd fallen all the way in love.

FOR THE SECOND TIME that month, Melanie stepped out on the moonlit veranda wearing a bridesmaid dress, intent on going after a man.

The same man.

She'd barely had a chance to exchange more than a few words with Marcus during the reception. There'd been too many relatives wanting to chat with both her and him, too many pictures to pose for. At one point when she'd finally found a moment when she wasn't surrounded, she went looking for Marcus only to find him involved in an intent conversation with her grandfather, her father and Demetri's father.

Just like at her cousin Shane's wedding, she'd decided to cut Marcus out of the pack right after her grandfather toasted the bride and groom. And in a déjà vu moment, the instant crystal flutes clinked together, Marcus set his empty glass aside and headed out the French doors.

This time, though, she knew he hadn't gone to what was now his former office. Since he planned on driving her back to Lucas Racing tomorrow, he was spending the night in the quarters where he'd lived while he worked at Quest.

Tightening her hands on the champagne bottle and two crystal flutes she'd snagged off the bar, Melanie paused at the steps leading down to the path that would take her to his quarters.

She'd had two days to think about this. Forty-eight hours to mull over what to do about Marcus. She hadn't had an answer until she walked down the aisle and turned to face the wedding guests. When her gaze settled on him, looking all dark and intense as he stood at the back of the conservatory, her chest had instantly tightened. She felt her palms begin to sweat against the stems of the flowers she held. Beneath her long gown, her legs turned wobbly.

If anyone had told her that the world could change in the single beat of a heart, she would have laughed. At that moment, though, she understood.

Because in that finger snap of time she realized that, somewhere along the line, the question of what to do about Marcus had stopped being hers to control.

It didn't matter whether she fully trusted him or not. It didn't matter what she knew about him, what she didn't know, what she thought she knew. All that mattered was being with him.

Dragging in a deep gulp of the chilly night air, Melanie headed down the steps and went after him.

HOW THE HELL many Prestons were there?

Marcus brooded over the question while using one foot to shove the door to the small apartment closed behind him. After jerking off his suit coat, he tossed it onto the nearest chair.

There'd been so many Prestons at the wedding reception, he'd begun to wonder if they had all of a sudden started coming out of the woodwork. Each time he got close to Melanie another member of her family appeared. Someone wanting to chat. Another someone tugging her away to pose for pictures with even more Prestons. It was enough to make a man grind glass with his teeth.

"Christ."

Jerking the knot of his tie loose, he stalked into the kitchen, his footsteps echoing hollowly against the empty walls and shelves. Without bothering to turn on the light, he crossed to the far counter, clamped both palms on the edge and stared out of the lone window over the sink.

All he could see was an unending darkness that matched his mood.

He had missed her these past two days. Missed seeing her, being with her. He'd dreamed about her, hot erotic dreams in which he'd tasted her, felt her. Each time he'd jolted awake to an empty bed, empty arms and furious frustration.

For the first time in his life, this morning—*Christmas morning*—had felt like more than just another day. Because of her. The ache of loss for all the Christmas mornings that fate had cheated him out of had kept his chest tight for hours.

His fingers gripped the edge of the counter harder when he thought about the promise he'd made to his dying mother. A promise he now bitterly regretted, but couldn't bring himself to break.

A promise that stood between him and the woman he loved.

Every hunter's instinct in him demanded he go find Melanie. Claim her. And to hell with the repercussions of his actions. He pictured his fingers sliding down the zipper of that sexy silver gown, peeling it off her body, then spreading her legs....

Frigging hell. He crushed the thought, because if he let himself finish it, the tenuous hold he had on his control would shatter.

A sharp rap on the door had him stalking back into

the living room. Wondering if there was a horde of Prestons on the front porch, he wrenched open the door. His heart lunged into his throat when he saw her there.

"What's your problem, Vasquez?" Melanie asked.

Gripping a bottle of champagne in one hand and crystal flutes in the other, she stood on the porch in a slice of moonlight that gave her satiny skin a silver radiance. His gaze slid down the length of the gown that hugged her curvy little body in all the right places. He refused to let himself think about how he'd imagined stripping all that soft, clingy fabric off her only moments before.

"Exactly which of my problems are you referring to?" he asked.

"The strange habit you have of taking off from a wedding reception immediately after the toasts are made. That isn't very friendly."

"I'm not in a friendly mood."

She tilted her head to the side. The cascade of stones at her ears caught the moonlight and glinted. "Does that mean you aren't thirsty?" she asked, holding up the bottle and flutes. "And that I should go away?"

He reached out, slid his hand around to cup the nape of her neck. "What I'm thirsty for isn't in that bottle." He felt a rush of savage satisfaction when her skin went hot against his fingers. "And going away would probably be a smart thing for you to do."

His touch, the husky timbre of his voice had Melanie swallowing hard. She knew he was right. But she'd already decided to damn the consequences. There were times when need, desire and lust simply overpowered logic. This was one of them.

"I don't feel much like being smart right now," she said softly.

"Don't say I didn't warn you," he muttered and tugged her inside. Kicking the door shut behind her, he settled his mouth on hers.

The kiss was exactly what she wanted. Hungry and fierce and mindless. His mouth was hot, and it was hard, and it was almost heathen as he crushed down to devour hers. She gave in to it, gave all to it, a moment's madness where body ruled mind and blood roared over reason.

She felt the champagne bottle slip from her fingers, heard the hollow *thunk* when it landed on the area rug.

Enough of her brain was still functioning that she dragged her mouth from his. "Let me get rid of these glasses," she whispered. She wiggled free of his hold and turned, but barely had time to set the crystal flutes on a nearby end table before he drew her back against him, nuzzling his lips at the nape of her neck.

"You don't know how long I've wanted to do this."

His hands were spread over her midsection where the pressure was coiled taut as a spring. "Since that night in your office when we kissed?" she breathed.

"Longer. I wanted you the first moment I saw you. You were sitting in the stables with your boots off, talking to Robbie."

"Marcus—" His name ended on a moan. His hands were over her breasts now, caressing, thumbs skimming, circling lightly over the peaks while his tongue did outrageous things to the back of her ear. Eyes closed, she relinquished any thought of control and arched back against him.

He used his teeth now, lightly grazing over her flesh while his hand moved to the neckline of her gown and he began to slide the zipper down. Her breathing slowed, deepened, like a woman in a trance. His tormenting fingertips barely brushed her spine as he unhurriedly opened the zipper.

"All night, I imagined what was under here." He spoke softly, close to her ear, and fought to keep his hands from taking too greedily.

Slowly, he parted the fabric, skimmed the gown down her body, then turned her into his arms.

"Holy…" he murmured, taking in the skin-caressing wisps of silver lace that molded her curves. "If I had known…" His voice hitched as his hand closed possessively over one firm breast. His thumb brushed across the nipple that budded hard and tight beneath lace. "If I'd known what was under that dress, I'd have hauled you out of the reception." He buried his face in her hair, drowning in its intoxicating scent as need slammed into him.

"You know now," she breathed while she jerked feverishly at the knot of his tie. Her hands trembled as she flipped open the buttons on his shirt.

Her fingers looked almost ghostlike splayed against his dark burnished chest. "I'm all yours, Marcus," she murmured while her fingertips made erotic patterns in the crisp black hairs.

He gritted his teeth when her hot, moist lips circled his nipple. She licked, suckled until he had to concentrate just to breathe.

He fought off his shirt, tossed it away, then cupped her

bottom and lifted. With her arms and legs wrapped around him like silken rope, he carried her toward the bedroom.

"Hurry." She nipped his jaw, then scraped her teeth down his throat while the word pumped like a pulse in his blood. *Hurry. Hurry.*

The small bedroom was dark and airy, lit by slashes of silver moonlight. He could see the silhouette of a bureau, desk and bookshelf. With Melanie clinging to him like a burr, he crossed the room, tumbling with her onto the bed.

If he'd gone insane with need, so had she. As though in silent agreement, neither gave thought to gentleness, to soft words or slow hands. They tore at each other, kicking off shoes, dragging off remaining clothing while feeding on each other with greedy kisses.

Rising over her, he kneed her thighs apart. He was keenly aware of every inch of her heated flesh, of every soft, supple curve, all there for his exploration and taking. Feeling a primitive need to conquer, to possess, he caught her wrists in one hand and stretched her arms over her head, arching her breasts upward. He dipped his head, suckled.

The feral purr that sounded in her throat went straight to his head like hot whiskey.

Their want of each other, *need* for each other was huge, ruthlessly keen. Right now, it was all that mattered.

To please her, and himself, he skimmed his free hand over her belly, down between her spread legs. He cupped her, found her wet and hot and unbearably arousing. *Mine,* he thought, hunger for her pumping inside him. His fingers plunged into her while he gorged himself on her flesh. Yet, when the fiery essence of her raced through his veins, he realized it was she who now possessed and conquered.

He was hers. From this moment on, he was hers.

Her breath strained as her head tossed restlessly back and forth within the frame of her upstretched arms. When she whispered his name, heat saturated him, as though a furnace door had been thrown open and the roaring blaze enveloped the room.

With his fingers impaling her, he could feel every pulse beat, hundreds of them, pounding in her. His thumb circled the bud between her thighs, an erotic massage of her throbbing flesh.

His fingers withdrew, entered her again, then again. Sweat slicked her compact curves; he felt her muscles tighten, the spasms boil swiftly upward.

"Again," he murmured. He sensed himself edging toward the boundaries of control while his fingers continued moving inside her. His thumb stroked her flesh until he shot her back up that slippery, heated path. When the second climax ripped through her, he shifted, braced himself over her.

She looked like a pagan goddess with her wild golden mane against the dark pillow and the sheen of moonlight on her damp skin.

"Look at me. Look at me, Melanie."

Her eyes fluttered open, drugged, sated and smoky blue.

"I want to see your eyes while I take you."

"Now, Marcus." Her lips trembled. "I want you inside me now."

She held his gaze as he thrust inside her, his heart crashing like thunder. He slid deeper, each move fueled by increasing urgency, increasing greed.

Need tore at him, clouding his mind, his vision. She arched higher to take him fully in, her hips meeting his, thrust for thrust as their bodies mated. Her muscles constricted around him at the same moment his body convulsed.

With the earth moving beneath him, he buried his face in her hair and surrendered himself to her.

MELANIE WOKE TO A DRAB morning-after-Christmas with weak light filtering through the curtains, the sound of rain pattering on the roof and a man wrapped around her.

Sated contentment swam through her as she turned her head and watched Marcus sleep.

He was sprawled on his side, one arm and leg tossed across her body in firm possession. The gray morning light splayed across his stubbled jaw and firm mouth; his dark hair was rumpled from the fingers she'd tunneled through it during the night.

On a swell of emotion, she knew with certainty she was undeniably, inexorably in love with Marcus Vasquez.

And yet, the nagging doubt remained that he hadn't been totally honest with her. Doubt that even now lay in her heart like a stone.

She couldn't, however, bring herself to regret becoming his lover.

What, she wondered, lay in their future? She skimmed a fingertip across Marcus's tousled hair while emotion tightened her throat. The hold he had on her was alternately comforting and frightening. She had been hurt before, terribly hurt by a man who'd lied to her about everything that mattered.

Taking a deep breath, she steadied herself. Marcus hadn't forced himself on her. She'd damned the consequences, and come to him.

She just had to hope that the only secrets left between them were the ones that didn't matter.

Chapter Twelve

The frigid rain and biting wind that settled over Kentucky the day after Christmas stuck like glue. It turned Lucas Racing's practice track muddy, soaking Melanie to the skin before the start of each training session and proving a blinding hazard thereafter. Having spent days dealing with flying mud, gloves slipping wetly on reins and waterlogged boots clinging to her feet, she sent up silent thanks when she and Marcus left for Florida.

And almost wept with joy when New Year's Day dawned to brilliant sunshine and palm trees swaying in the warm breeze.

Gulfstream Park kicked off the road to the Kentucky Derby with the Gulf Classic, the first important race of the year. Reporters representing television, newspapers and magazines all clamored for features and interviews. To appease the media, the Florida course sponsored an annual press reception on New Year's morning, only hours before the race.

With his hand on her elbow, Marcus nudged Melanie into a small alcove just outside the door to the race club lounge. He looked down at her, his eyes dark, unreadable pools. "Before we go in, I want to tell you that I know how hard you've worked for this day. You deserve to win."

"So do you." She gazed into his gorgeous face, and instantly felt the heat moving up from her toes. "When we went by his stall in the receiving barn this morning, Something To Talk About gave me a hot tip on the race."

Marcus angled his chin. "Sorry I missed that. What was the tip?"

"Even though he's feeling a little homesick, he intends to win today."

"Is that so?"

She nodded. "And when he does, it won't be just for Lucas Racing. It'll be for Quest, too."

"Do you plan to announce to the media that if Something To Talk About crosses the finish line first, it won't be any of your doing? That you're just going along for the ride?"

She flashed him a look through her lashes. "I'm keeping that between us."

His eyes softened as he took her chin in his hand. "Here's something else that's between us," he murmured as his mouth lowered to hers.

He kissed her slowly, gently and with the utmost concentration.

Instantly, she was swamped by the taste, the texture, the heat. His scent seduced her senses. His name was a murmur on her lips, a whisper in her mind. As with each time he touched her, she knew that no man had ever filled her so quickly, so completely, so utterly to the exclusion of all else.

"Marcus." She pressed her palm against his chest, and eased back. She couldn't get her breath, but she could hear it, feel it coming slow and heavy through her lips. Her whole body was tingling, yet he was barely touching her. "This isn't exactly the best time or place for this." Against her palm she felt his heart pounding in rhythm with hers.

"Maybe not." He ran his hands down the arms of the trim black jacket she'd paired with an above-the-knee skirt. "It's going to be a zoo in there with all the media. When your interviews are over, you have to go change and weigh in for the race. This might be the only time I have with you for a while. I wanted you to know I'll be thinking about you. And make sure you'll be thinking about me."

She struggled to even her breathing. "After that kiss, you've got nothing to worry about."

His hands went still against her arms. But he *did* have something to worry about, Marcus thought. So much so that he'd left their bed every night since they'd become lovers and paced the floor while she slept. He had made a promise to his mother. A deathbed promise. Just the thought of breaking the vow he'd sworn so long ago had filled him with racking guilt.

Now, as he stood there, gazing down into Melanie's blue eyes, what had seemed hopelessly complicated was suddenly painfully simple. His mother had demanded the promise from him out of hate for the man who'd scorned her. But Melanie represented love and all the good things he'd never had in life. It was time he made his own choices, not be driven by his mother's.

It was time to tell Melanie the truth.

"There is something I need to tell you," he said quietly. "After the race, we have to talk."

Melanie felt a prick of apprehension at the somber tone that had settled so suddenly in his voice. She'd known something was bothering him. After they'd become lovers, they had spent their nights together. And each night she'd woken and reached for him, only to find him gone. She'd lain in the dark, listening to him in the living room, pacing. And each day, disappointment had drowned her small burst of hope that he would confide in her.

Now, it seemed, he was ready.

"Tell me now," she urged softly.

"Later." He lifted her hand, pressed his lips to her palm. "After the race."

"All right." She closed her eyes for a moment, centered herself mentally. "Ready to hit the media zoo?"

"Ready."

Inside, the lounge was packed, the decibel level high. Glasses of orange juice sprouted from many a fist. Including Brent Preston's.

"Brent!" Melanie exclaimed when she spotted her

brother. Standing on tiptoe, she kissed his cheek. "Why didn't you tell us you were planning on coming to Florida?"

"It was a spur-of-the-moment thing," Brent said while shaking Marcus's hand. "Despite Quest's current problems, I need to keep up to date on the serious contenders in all races. A lot of Thorough-breds wind up as breeders eventually." He looked with suspicious concentration at his glass. "Besides, Dad and Mom thought it would be a good idea for me to show up here."

Melanie arched a brow. Over the entire Christmas holiday, she'd been aware of the concern she'd seen in her parents' eyes whenever they looked at her. "Does your assignment also include keeping an eye on your baby sister?"

Brent took a swig of orange juice and gave her a benign smile. "Seems like I remember something along those lines. When you got grabbed by that guy with the knife, it shook us all up." He shrugged. "Look at it this way. You're my personal Christmas shopper. If something happened to you, I'd be in a real jam with my twins."

"Heaven forbid," Melanie said drily, then squeezed his hand. "Thanks for being here."

"Don't mention it."

Shifting away from Brent, she took in their surround-ings. She recognized numerous sportswriters moving and mingling through the crowd, all looking for exclu-sives, ears stretching to hear conversations behind them. Trainers held small conferences, the press heads bend-ing to catch vital words. Owners stood around looking either smug or bemused according to how often they'd attended this sort of gathering.

In one corner of the room, several of her fellow jockeys stood before cameras, giving interviews. Melanie figured her turn would come soon.

"Brent, did you hear back from Detective Quinn?" Marcus asked. "Does he know where Carl Suarez was when he called Melanie?" They had learned later that Carl had called Melanie first at Lucas Racing, where the head groom told him she'd gone to Quest for her dad's birthday.

"All the police could find out was that Carl was somewhere in the southern part of Georgia."

"Georgia?" Melanie frowned. "That day he came to me he said he was headed for his aunt's house in Mexico."

"Apparently he changed his mind," Brent said. "Or someone changed it for him. Bottom line is, the police have no idea where the kid is."

"What about the bastard who shot Carl's father?" Marcus asked, his palm settling against the small of Melanie's back. "And probably attacked your sister? Any word on him?"

"Quinn ran the killer's tattoo through several law enforcement databases. Nothing came up."

"Excuse me, Miss Preston, several reporters would like an interview with you." The woman who spoke was tall and thin, and wore a laminated ID issued by the racetrack clipped to the lapel of a lightweight blazer. She nodded toward the far side of the lounge where cameras were set up. "Over there."

"Lead the way." Melanie squeezed Marcus's arm. "Be back in a few."

The various interviews she gave stretched to nearly half an hour. When Melanie finished with the last reporter, she excused her way back to the area of the lounge where she'd left Marcus and Brent. Being only five feet tall in a room filled with what felt like Amazons, she considered it a miracle when she spotted her brother.

"Have you seen Marcus?" she asked, sidling up to Brent.

"Last time was about twenty minutes ago. He was deep in conversation with a couple of other trainers." While he spoke, Brent swept his gaze over the crowd. "There he is," he said after a moment. "Over by the open doors leading out to the veranda."

Melanie shifted, spotted Marcus. She was too far away to read his expression, but beneath his suit coat his shoulders looked rigid. He made a curt gesture in the direction of the veranda, then waited for a tall man with thinning brown hair to step outside ahead of him. Marcus followed.

She looked at Brent. "Do you know who that man is?"

"Nolan Hunter."

"The owner of Apollo's Ice?" she asked, blinking.

"The one and only." Brent slid a hand into the pocket of his slacks. "I didn't see anyone introduce Marcus to Hunter. They just started talking, like they've met before." Brent's forehead creased into a frown. "Mel, has Marcus ever mentioned that he knows the viscount?"

"No." A little twinge at the base of Melanie's spine told her something was wrong. Just...wrong. "It's news to me."

KEEPING HIS FACE a neutral mask, Marcus stepped through the doors and onto the veranda. With dread splashing through his gut like acid, he could almost feel the secrets of his past on a march to the present. All week he'd grappled with the twin forces that pulled at him from opposite directions. He'd made a promise to his dying mother, yet keeping his word prevented him from being completely honest with the woman he loved. So, he had decided to tell Melanie the truth. After the race.

As he paused on the breezy, sunlit veranda where only a few other people stood, he had a feeling, a very *sick* feeling, that he'd waited too long.

Jaw clenched, he studied the half brother he hadn't seen in ten years, and discovered a lot had changed. Nolan Hunter's wiry build had turned beefy enough that the weight gain couldn't be camouflaged by his impeccably tailored tweed jacket. His once thick brown hair had thinned, and deep lines were etched at the corners of his eyes. Time, Marcus thought, had not been kind to the viscount.

"What are you doing here, Hunter?"

"Is that any way to greet me after a decade?"

"I asked what you're doing here," Marcus repeated.

"And I might inquire the same thing about you." Hunter's deep voice and proper BBC accent hadn't changed. All so polite. Still, even after ten years, Marcus clearly remembered the outraged tirade that had turned Hunter's face crimson and his accented words into a snarl. That tirade had been fueled by Marcus's mother's request to see their father one last time.

"I have a horse running in this race," Marcus said.

"As do I. Sterling Pass."

Marcus pulled the race statistics he'd studied for weeks from his brain. Hunter's name hadn't shown up anywhere. "You're not listed as an owner."

"I just bought shares in the stallion the day before yesterday, so there wasn't time to add my name to the printed materials. No matter, I was already in the States on other business, so I decided to see my new investment race."

Loathing. It was liquid and cold, like mercury flowing through Marcus's veins. "Does that other business have anything to do with Apollo's Ice?"

"Oh, dear, that *is* an unfortunate situation. Let me assure you I am as puzzled as everyone else over what went wrong at the Angelina Stud Farm."

"A vet who worked at Angelina at that time may have been murdered," Marcus said levelly, "and a horse supposedly sired by Apollo's Ice was poisoned in Dubai. Turned out your horse wasn't in fact the real sire—just like Leopold's Legacy."

Hunter blinked. "Surely you're not suggesting I had anything to do with the DNA mix-up or, God forbid, a man's murder?"

"I'm suggesting it's possible," Marcus said.

"That's absurd. I know nothing about what went on at Angelina."

"As far as I'm concerned, the jury's still out on that."

Hunter touched his fingertips to his perfectly knotted tie, taking a moment to visibly calm himself.

"Marcus, I understand your animosity toward me. I don't exactly feel brotherly affection toward you, either.

But don't you see the folly in your trying to make me look guilty of something simply because our father refused to acknowledge you as his? One has nothing to do with the other."

The overheard remark caught Melanie like a slap in the face as she stepped abreast of Marcus. *"Your father?"*

Her startled gasp had Marcus whipping his head in her direction. Their eyes locked for an instant, then he turned away. He couldn't have looked more guilty if she'd caught him with a hooker.

Dread slithered up her spine. She confronted Nolan Hunter. "You two are *brothers?*"

"My dear, since Marcus doesn't seem prepared to introduce us, allow me to do so for him," the Englishman said while extending his hand. "I am Nolan Hunter."

Up close, Melanie studied the tall man whose looks and limp handshake could only be described as underwhelming. His face was pale, his eyes a muddy brown color, as was his thinning hair. She saw absolutely nothing comparable between Nolan Hunter's wanness and Marcus's dark Mediterranean good looks.

"And you are?"

Hunter's question jerked her thoughts back. "Melanie Preston."

"Of course, the famous jockey." Both Hunter's smile and voice warmed. "I should have recognized you from your racing photos. May I congratulate you on your wins at the Derby and Preakness?"

"Thank you." She bit back the impatience that came

from the need to talk to Marcus alone. She wanted an explanation.

"It was so unfortunate that your family had to pull Leopold's Legacy from competing in the Belmont. I've spoken several times to your brother, Brent, and have assured him that I, like everyone else, believed that Apollo's Ice sired Legacy. I'm appalled by the unfortunate circumstances that have caused your family so much trouble."

"Appalled is the correct term," she agreed and set her jaw. She wanted her question answered. "You two are brothers?" she repeated.

"Half brothers," Marcus ground out. "This is the second time we've ever seen each other."

"Yes," Nolan agreed. "I'm afraid circumstances were such that my sister Devon and I grew up apart from Marcus." Nolan glanced toward the far end of the veranda where a stately dressed couple stood. "My friends are waiting, so I must go. I wish you luck in the race, Miss Preston, even though you're riding against Sterling Pass."

"He's yours?"

"I own a mere few shares." Instead of extending his hand toward Marcus, Hunter gave him a curt nod. "Marcus, perhaps we'll run into each other again under more favorable circumstances."

Melanie curled her hands into fists as she watched the man turn and walk away. He paused, said something to the waiting couple, then they stepped into the race lounge, leaving her and Marcus alone on the veranda where pots filled with flowers spilled color and scent across the marble floor.

"Melanie—"

She whirled to face him. "Why didn't you tell me you and Nolan Hunter are brothers?"

"Half brothers," he clarified. "And that's what I wanted to talk to you about after the race."

"Oh, really? What convenient timing." It wasn't just anger Marcus heard in her voice, but pain. He could have withstood the anger.

"There's nothing convenient about it," he countered, trying to keep the panic he felt out of his voice. "I told you about the promise I made to my mother not to reveal to anyone the name of the man who fathered me and shunned us both. I made that promise with the intention of keeping it."

"You promised not to tell anyone," Melanie repeated, her voice carrying a perceptible quake. "You *slept* with me, Marcus. I would have thought that made me more than just 'anyone.' Clearly I was wrong."

"Melanie." He started toward her, only to be brought up short when her hands whipped out.

"Don't." Why hadn't she listened to that nagging voice inside of her that cautioned not to get involved with him? Not to let the barriers down she'd erected around her heart. "I told you how I feel about secrets. If yours was so precious, so *unrevealable,* why didn't you just stay away from me?"

"I tried, from the very first time I laid eyes on you." His hands fell uselessly to his sides. "For the entire time I worked at Quest, I fought the pull I felt toward you."

"Not hard enough."

"No." His fingers curled tight into his palms. "My last night at Quest, when you came to my office to tell me goodbye, I kissed you because I could no longer help myself. I thought it would be the last time I saw you."

"Then why offer me a job?"

"Because you're the best damn jockey around."

She felt her throat constrict. "Sleeping with me was just a bonus?"

"No," he said fiercely. "I didn't want our relationship to be about anything except work, but the more time I spent with you, the more I wanted to know you. Work with you. *Be* with you." He looked at her, standing in the bright sunlight, her face pale. The tears glinting in her eyes nearly undid him. "Instead, I hurt you."

He took a step toward her, and held himself back from reaching for her. He wanted to hold her. Lift her against him, touch her hair, her skin, and convince himself everything would be fine. "I'm sorry," he said, struggling against waves of guilt and need.

"Why are you sorry? You kept your promise to your mother. You didn't tell me."

"I *couldn't* tell you, not at first."

"Not at first. Not even when you slept with me." As long as she kept her brain cold, Melanie told herself, she could think. She could think and not feel. "You made that choice, Marcus."

"I told you more about myself, my past, than I've ever told anyone," he shot back, fighting desperation. "I did that because you matter. Because I fell in love with you. I love you, Melanie."

"You know what? My ex-lover, the cop, told me that same thing a couple of hours before his very pregnant secret confronted me in the mall parking lot."

Digging deep, Marcus found his control again. "I handled this all wrong. You're the one person I should have been open with. I never meant to hurt you."

"You did a good job, regardless." She jabbed a hand through her hair. "All along, I *knew* you were holding something back, that I'd be wrong to trust you. But I finally just shoved that out of my mind, took a leap of faith." She could feel pain ripping through her, and with it came a realization. "Apollo's Ice," she said. "Your half brother owns the horse that has put my family on the edge of disaster. Did you believe I would think you're somehow involved in this whole mess? By association, if for no other reason?"

"How could you *not* think that?" Restraint gone, Marcus gripped her arms. "I've done nothing but profit from the nightmare your family is embroiled in. Because of it, Demetri pulled his horses from Quest and opened a competing stable. He made me his full partner, we now own the majority shares of the colt your family counted on to be its saving grace, and their former champion jockey is about to ride that horse in a race for our stables. In a few years, Lucas Racing will be everything Quest once was. All thanks to the scandal centered around the stallion owned by my half brother."

He held her still when she would have stepped back. "If you had known I was related to Hunter, you would have thought of all that. Wondered about my intentions. You would have never let me near you."

Her blue eyes snapped. "Don't tell me what I would have thought! What I would have done." She jerked from his hold. "Don't you understand, Marcus? This isn't about the promise you made to your mother. Or whom you're related to. This is all about trust. I made the decision to trust you. You should have done the same for me."

When an announcement blared over the sound system, she took a small but significant step backward, away from him. "I've got to go change."

"We'll talk about this later." The certainty he could never make things right, that he'd lost her ripped through him. "After the race."

She said nothing, just turned and walked away.

WHILE MELANIE CHANGED CLOTHES, then went through the racecourse's official weigh-in, she consciously refused to acknowledge the empty, aching, miserable pain in her heart. The race ahead, the taxing job facing her had absolute priority. Although it took a massive effort of will, she moved the confrontation with Marcus to the back of her mind. There was too much at stake, and she was too much of a professional, to let her personal anguish color the outcome of a race she'd trained so hard for. At this moment, she was solely Melanie Preston, jockey, some years champion, some years not, hoping to be champion again.

Wearing Lucas Racing's crimson-and-silver silks for the first time and carrying the saddle she'd been required to weigh in with, she walked out of the weighing room toward the parade ring.

As Something To Talk About's trainer, Marcus stood

waiting for her there. If almost by silent agreement, he made no attempt to color their prerace conversation with anything personal.

"You'll win," he said, nudging the saddle from her hands.

"With luck," she added.

Led by the groom Marcus had handpicked to travel with the colt, Something To Talk About cantered around the ring. He held his gray head high, the crimson rug with *LR* embroidered in silver thread covering all else from withers to tail.

The groom removed the rug with a practiced flick of the wrist, then took the saddle from Marcus. Minutes later, the signal sounded for the jockeys to mount. The groom turned to give Melanie a leg up into the saddle.

Marcus stepped in. "I'll do it."

"Yes, sir."

With so many people around, Melanie didn't protest. Just closed her eyes when he leaned in and the woodsy fragrance of his aftershave enveloped her. Instantly, she felt the pull. *He loved her.* He had told her he loved her. Yet, she knew all too well that without trust, love meant little.

While she gathered the reins and slid her booted feet into the irons, Marcus settled his hand on her calf and squeezed.

"I made a mistake and I'm truly sorry." His voice was calm and quiet, negating any remote possibility of being overheard. "Please say we can talk after this."

Her lips trembled, but she firmed them against a sob. As if sensing her distress, Something To Talk About shied under her, and danced in a fretful half circle before she thought to control him.

Her hands shook.

She forced her mind to the competition ahead, taking slow and deliberate breaths until her pulse rate steadied. In silence, she reined the colt out of the parade ring.

AS THEY APPROACHED the starting gate, Something To Talk About's eyes were liquid clear, his ears pricked upward, his muscles quivering to be off. Melanie knew that to the masses of people watching from the stands, he was a picture of a taut, tuned racing machine eager to get on with the job he was born for.

While the other jockeys adjusted their helmets and goggles, Melanie slipped off one glove, leaned forward and placed her palm against the flat of the colt's cheek. It was warm and soft and she could feel the tiny twitch of jaw muscles near the base of his head.

"Okay, big boy, this is it," she crooned. "You and I are going out there and kicking major butt. When you hit the finish line first, every mare from here to Kentucky is going to know you are one hot stud."

As if in agreement, Something To Talk About tossed his massive gray head.

In the next heartbeat, she felt the slow pumping rhythm which she recognized as the colt's inbred will to race and win. It seemed to surge through his blood like a song, then pour straight into her.

Minutes later, all horses had been loaded into the gates. With a ringing clang, they sprang open. Something To Talk About set off with a fierce burst of speed.

Body forward, knees bent almost up to her chin, Melanie held the colt back gradually with hands and mind. Where it was Something To Talk About's job to run, it was hers to control the speed, to hold it on simmer, to wait.

And keep her eye on the competition.

As usual, traffic jams occurred along the rail, so Melanie kept Something To Talk About skimming down the outside. After battling for more than half a mile, the two front-running horses grew tired. Sterling Pass—Nolan Hunter's stallion—had been bottled up behind them. He moved around the former leaders and found clear space to run in.

When they reached the last bend, Melanie tightened her legs, sending Something To Talk About the message that it was time to get on with it.

Beneath her, he surged down the backstretch, running neck and neck with Sterling Pass.

Melanie eased her body forward, shifting all of her weight off the colt's spine onto his powerful shoulders. "This is what it's all about, your future, take it, embrace it, it's all yours," she said over the hammering thrum of hooves. At the last minute, Something To Talk About shed Sterling Pass like dead leaves.

Both Melanie and the colt were bursting with pride when she pulled him up. The crowd in the stands was on its feet, cheering.

The ecstatic groom took the reins, led them into the winners' enclosure, a curtain call for a smash hit.

"He earned that win," Marcus said over the din of noise. "So did you."

Melanie had sat astride numerous winners before. Had received blankets of flowers, trophies, smiled for pictures with trainers and owners. The pain in her heart, however, made today's win bittersweet.

Marcus stepped away from a clutch of reporters long enough to say, "After you weigh in and change, we need to talk. Please."

She nearly gave in. Very nearly. There was as much misery in his eyes as she was holding inside her. But she needed time to herself to think. To figure out what her true feelings were beneath all the roiling emotion.

"Not here," she said quietly. "Not until we get back to Lucas Racing."

A muscle in his jaw twitched. "We're not going back until tomorrow."

"I've made other arrangements. I saw some long-time friends of my parents here earlier. They flew in on their private jet and said I'm welcome to hitch a ride back to Kentucky with them this evening. That's what I'm going to do."

Marcus's eyes narrowed. "Then what?"

"I don't know. I need time to sort things out."

A reporter stepped up just then and asked Marcus a question. Melanie used the moment to ease away.

Like all other jockeys, she was required to report to the clerk of the scales to weigh in not just immediately before a race, but after. She slid the loop of her riding crop over one wrist, then accepted the saddle the beaming groom had tugged off Something To Talk About. While the groom led the colt away to cool off, Melanie received another round of congratulations.

Moments later, she headed in the direction of the weighing room.

With the race over, the crowd had thinned considerably. The closer she got to the jockeys' area, the fewer people there were milling around. And the more thoughts of Marcus closed in on her.

If she'd been paying attention, if she hadn't been thinking about Marcus, perhaps she would have sensed the man closing in on her sooner. But her mind was elsewhere as she walked past the dim corridor that led to the racecourse's underground mechanical systems.

As it was, she had only seconds to feel her skin prickle with fear, a brief instant for her fingers to clench the saddle, before the dark figure leaped at her from the corridor.

The shriek that rose up her throat ended in a gurgle when he jerked her backward.

Chapter Thirteen

As if she were weightless, the man slammed Melanie backward against the wall of the dimly lit corridor. The impact knocked the wind out of her. Her ears started ringing and stars burst before her eyes.

"Where's the kid?"

"Kid?" she panted. With her vision still blurred, the man was no more than a burly figure.

His hand whipped up. The knife blade, gleaming wicked and deadly in the dim light, cleared all of her senses. "Carl Suarez."

The familiar, thickly accented voice and remembered smell of pine cologne sent her mind racing with the potent fuel of panic. This was the man who had attacked her in the stables at Lucas Racing.

"I...don't know where...Carl is." Fear was like a

living thing, wrapping its tentacles around her throat. *You survived the first time. You can make it out alive again.*

He jabbed the knife blade toward her chest. "He called you from Atlanta. He's on his way here. Or already here. *Where is he?*"

"I...don't...know."

Her attacker was big and close, looming over her. Melanie felt a drop of perspiration slide down between her breasts. There *had* to be a way out, a way to fight back. The alternative was too terrible to contemplate.

She flicked a look toward the entrance to the corridor, only a few feet away. The race had been over long enough that all of the patrons had either left the track or were on their way out. Probably the majority of the course's employees and vendors, too. She couldn't just stand there and count on some passerby to help.

If she still had her saddle, she could maybe use it as a shield against the knife long enough to get away. But the saddle had fallen from her grasp when the man grabbed her and it was somewhere beyond the entrance to the corridor.

When he brandished the knife in her face, she cringed...and felt something bump against the side of her leg. Only then did she realize she still had the strap of her riding crop looped around her right wrist.

Swallowing hard, she curled her clammy, trembling fingers around its hard leather handle.

"You're right. Carl...called me...from Atlanta." Her voice was shaking as badly as her hands, but she had to talk. If she could buy herself enough time, maybe she would find an opening to use the crop. "The connection was awful, I could barely hear him," she added. "I told him to go to the police. I don't know if he did or not."

"You lying *bitch!* I tracked him here!" the man dropped his voice and she could feel the force of his words against her cheek. He wasn't touching her, but the blade glinting inches from her eyes kept her frozen in place. "Suarez is somewhere at this racetrack. He has the pictures his father took."

"I don't—"

"Melanie!"

There would be times, countless times later, when she would look back and remember that moment. The way the gleaming blade remained inches from her face when her attacker's head jerked toward the sound of Marcus's voice. The fearlessness in Marcus's eyes when he stepped into view, his mouth grim, his gaze locked on her assailant.

With his head tilted toward the light shining at the end of the corridor, Melanie got her first good look at her assailant's eyes. They were empty. Dead. It was like staring into the window of a vacant house.

Her eyes flicked back to his knife hand. And then she saw it, the small rectangle tattooed on the inside of his wrist. A line cut diagonally through it, one half of the rectangle red, the other half gold. Melanie felt something click in her mind, but it faded against the marrow-deep terror that came with the confirmation this man had murdered Santos Suarez and maybe the Irish vet. She doubted he would hesitate to kill again.

And Marcus was currently inching his way closer.

Going purely on instinct, she jerked her arm up, slashed the riding crop against the side of the man's head. He howled; blood spurted across her chest as he staggered sideways, the vicious blade still clutched in his hand.

"Knife!" she screamed.

She didn't know if Marcus heard her before he rammed into the guy dead-on sideways. Her attacker's back hit the wall, then he lunged toward Marcus. All Melanie could see were bodies pitching and tossing, everything hazy in the uneven light.

"Melanie, get out!" Marcus shouted at her. "Run!"

The fear barreling through her like a locomotive kept her frozen in place.

Marcus pivoted, gripped the man's knife hand at the wrist. They stumbled sideways toward the entrance to the corridor, straining against each other, their faces close, the smell of sweat and blood and violence fouling the air.

Melanie caught light glinting off the blade as it inched closer to Marcus. The lethal point was nearly under his chin while the men swayed together, their bodies knocking against the cement walls.

"No!" In a mindless, animal movement, she leaped onto the attacker's back, sobbing, cursing as she struck the handle of the crop against his head. He staggered and sent Marcus stumbling backward out of the corridor.

With a howl of pain, the man threw her off. Melanie's head rapped hard against the wall, replaying the same stars dancing before her eyes. Adrenaline firing through her system, she scrambled to her feet, lashing out with the riding crop as she advanced on the bastard with a vengeance.

It was Marcus who pulled her away, shoved her out of the path of the blade that whistled by her face.

"Get out!" he shouted, and pushed her out of the corridor.

Then he lunged, sending both him and his quarry crashing to the ground. They grappled on the floor, panting like dogs. The uppermost thought in Marcus's mind was to see Melanie safe. But his hands were slippery with blood and he couldn't gain a firm hold on the man.

Using all of his strength, he twisted the bastard's hand, veering the knife away from his own heart. With a burst of adrenaline, he plunged the blade into the attacker's chest.

When Marcus rolled weakly upright, he knew it was over.

"Marcus!" He looked across his shoulder in time to see Melanie limping toward him, sobbing his name. She dropped to her knees beside him and his heart stopped when he saw the blood that spattered her chest.

He managed to lift a hand to her shoulder. "You're hurt! How bad are you hurt?"

"It's not my blood," she said, her voice a thin, shaky thread.

"Thank God." He tightened his fingers on her shoulder. If he could have managed it, he'd have shaken her. "You want to tell me what the hell you thought you were doing, jumping on the bastard's back that way?"

"Did you expect me to just stand by and watch you get stabbed in the throat?"

Her fingers shook as they fought to loosen the knot

of his tie. "You're bleeding. How bad are you hurt? Your arm's bleeding. Your head."

"I'm all right," he said through clenched teeth. His jaw clamped tighter when she wrapped the tie around his biceps, tourniquet style, and the burning in his arm shot to blast furnace mode.

"What the hell?"

Marcus looked up, saw a narrow-eyed security guard easing in, gun drawn. "He attacked Miss Preston," Marcus said, gesturing his chin toward the dead man. "You need to call the police."

"Ambulance." Melanie swallowed around the knot in her throat. "Call an ambulance first."

The guard holstered his weapon, whipped out his radio.

"Marcus, I'm sorry. I'm so sorry." She wanted to lay her head on his shoulder and sob, just sob. But she continued using the loose ends of the tie to dab at the blood flowing from the scrape on his temple.

"Sorry?" He dragged in a breath, eased it out. "This wasn't exactly your fault."

"He almost killed you." Tears swam in her blue eyes. "You took him on to save me, and he almost killed you."

The security guard's cell phone rang. He answered the call, listened for a moment, then looked at Melanie. "Miss Preston, another guard is bringing your brother here. He's got a kid named Carl Suarez with him."

Melanie nodded as she continued dabbing at Marcus's temple. "The man knew," she told Marcus. "He said he tracked Carl here. He thought Carl had some pictures and was meeting me."

"Pictures of what?"

"I don't know."

"Melanie!" Brent raced in, Carl Suarez beside him.

Melanie watched her brother assess her and Marcus, then catch sight of the dead man. His face paled. "Christ."

Brent crouched beside her, one hand cupping her cheek. "Are you okay?"

"I am, but Marcus isn't. He needs an ambulance. Can you check with the guard?"

"It's just a scratch," Marcus countered. One that burned like hell, he conceded silently.

"Your head's bleeding," she said. "Your arm's bleeding. You have to go to the E.R."

As if to reassure himself that she was uninjured, he settled his hand on her thigh. "I don't need a damn hospital."

"I'll check on the ambulance anyway." Brent gave Carl's shoulder a squeeze. "Be right back."

Melanie extended a hand toward the young man. "Are you okay?"

Gripping her hand, Carl squatted beside them. "I… Yeah, I'm good."

Melanie noted he was wearing the same clothes he'd had on weeks ago when she'd last seen him. The jacket she'd given him was streaked with dirt, as was his face, bare of the silver ring that had pierced his left eyebrow. She estimated he'd lost a good ten pounds.

Carl's gaze flicked to the lifeless body. "Is that the man who shot my father?"

"Yes, I saw the tattoo on his wrist." Melanie furrowed her forehead. "That tattoo, it reminded me of something."

"What?" Marcus asked.

She struggled to pull back the memory, but her mind was reeling and she was too shaky to concentrate. "I don't know."

"I want to look at the tattoo." Carl's mouth quivered as he rose. "I'm gonna make sure it was the same one I saw."

When Melanie opened her mouth to protest, Marcus squeezed her thigh.

"He needs to look." He winced as she continued to dab at the scrape on his temple. "The bastard's been tracking Carl around the country for weeks. The kid'll probably have nightmares unless he sees for himself that it's the same tattoo and the guy is really dead."

"You're right." Melanie watched Carl approach the man's lifeless body, the arm outstretched so that she had a clear view of the tattoo. "I remember now," she said as realization swept over her.

"Remember what?" Marcus asked.

"When I rode Something To Talk About at the Sandstone Derby in Dubai, one of the other jockeys wore silks that had the same red-and-gold pattern as that man's tattoo." She glanced across her shoulder. "I need to tell Brent about the tattoo. And find out where the…

"Finally!" she exclaimed when two uniformed EMTs rushed in. "He needs to go to the hospital," she said as she scooted out of their way.

"You said the same thing when I got kicked by that filly," Marcus grated as one of the EMTs cut the sleeve of his suit coat and shirt with one quick slice. "I didn't need to go to the hospital then and I don't need to go now."

THE EMTS AGREED WITH MARCUS. They finished patching his wounds just as the police arrived. After cordoning off the crime scene, a uniformed officer escorted all involved parties into the racetrack's lounge.

Two hours later, they were still there.

Wearing the clean shirt one of the security guards had lent him, Marcus sat at a large round table, his right temple covered by a gauze pad. Butterfly bandages secured the cut on his upper arm, which still burned like summer in Death Valley.

He glanced at Melanie in the chair beside his and narrowed his eyes. It seemed to him she was even paler than she'd been before she'd gone to the jockeys' area where she'd changed back into her black, trim suit. It would be a long time before the image of her, dressed in blood-spattered silks, faded from his mind.

Across the room, Brent Preston stood with his cell phone to his ear, his expression grim. It had been equally grim moments before when Marcus briefed him about his blood link to Nolan Hunter. To be fair, Marcus had emphasized that there was no evidence to back up his suspicions that Hunter hadn't been totally up front about the scandal.

"Overall, this is quite a story." The comment came from Isaac Young, a tall, balding homicide detective. Instantly on his arrival he had begun conducting interviews. Then he spent a half hour on the phone with Detective Quinn, who'd briefed him on the homicide of Santos Suarez in Kentucky.

"Son, you're lucky to be alive," Young said, addressing Carl Suarez. "I imagine after spending weeks on the run, you know that you should have stayed put and called the police, like Miss Preston wanted you to do."

"Yes, sir," Carl said from the chair beside Melanie's. "I was just so scared that the man who killed my dad would come after me."

"Well, you were right about that," Young said, referring to his notes. "According to the passport we found on him, his name is Zakir Alanssi. Interpol has a file on him. Although he isn't wanted at the moment for any specific crime, it's believed Alanssi is a professional killer."

"Any idea who he's working for?" Marcus asked.

"Not yet," Young said. "His passport was issued by the United Arab Emirates. It lists him as a resident of Dubai."

"Which goes along with what I remembered about his tattoo,"

Melanie said.

"Which was?" Young asked.

"A couple of months ago, I raced in the Sandstone Derby in Dubai. One of the other jockeys in that race wore silks that had the same red-and-gold pattern as Alanssi's tattoo."

Young looked at Brent, who'd just completed his phone call and slid into a chair beside Carl. "Is the DNA fraud you briefed me on connected to Dubai?"

Brent nodded, his blue eyes grim. "A horse believed to have been sired by Apollo's Ice was poisoned there. Test results confirmed that the dead horse and Leopold's Legacy were sired by the same mystery stallion."

"Who owned the poisoned horse?" Young asked.

"An English lord named Harrison Rochester. That's

who I just got off the phone with. When I told him about Alanssi's tattoo and the matching jockey's silks that Melanie remembered, Rochester told me the man the jockey rode for has ties to gambling networks in London. Rochester is going to see what he can find out about those networks, then get back to me."

Young nodded. "We'll be pursuing that same line of investigation, but I'd appreciate you keeping me updated on what you find. Now," he continued, shifting his attention back to Carl. "Alanssi mentioned to Miss Preston that he was after you because you had pictures he wanted. Any idea what those might be?"

"No." Carl's dark brows slid together. "I don't know about any pictures."

Melanie gripped his hand. "Carl, what about the cell phone your father gave you right after Alanssi forced your car off the road? The pictures he was after might be some your dad took on his cell phone. Do you still have it?"

"I kept it for a few days, but since it was busted, I got rid of it. Tossed it in some river." Carl's expression was stricken. "You think maybe I threw away evidence that could prove why my dad was murdered?"

Brent settled a hand on the boy's shoulder. "We'll find all the answers we need. Eventually." He looked at Young. "If you're done with us, Detective, I'll take Carl back to my hotel. I imagine he'd like to clean up before I buy him the biggest steak I can find in Florida."

Carl's mouth curved. "I expect I could eat an entire cow."

"Then you and Mr. Preston better be on your way." Young flipped the cover of his notepad closed. "I'm done with everyone. Mr. Vasquez, we're more than satisfied that you killed Alanssi in self-defense. I don't think your presence will be required at the inquest into his death, but if that changes, I'll get in touch with you at Lucas Racing."

"I'll be there," Marcus said.

As the detective walked away, Marcus placed a palm beneath Melanie's elbow and nudged her up with him. "There are some things I need to say to you before you take off. Please let me say them."

She gazed up into Marcus's face. He had cuts, scrapes and bruises, yet she knew they weren't the reason for the misery in his eyes. She was.

Her fingers curled into her palms as she pictured him grappling with Alanssi. She could still hear the echoing thud of fists, the crack of bone on bone. The titanic jittery fear that gripped her when the knife's blade angled toward Marcus's throat had turned her pulse permanently ragged.

And given her a preview of what her life would be without him.

"All right," she said softly.

He turned, spotted the security guard who'd lent him the shirt. "Mind if we use the veranda for a few minutes?"

The guard shrugged. "Not a problem. I'm working the night shift, so take your time."

"Thanks."

After making sure Brent had Carl firmly under his wing, Melanie stepped with Marcus out onto the veranda, now bathed in evening shadow. She knew it had only been hours since they stood there before the race, yet it seemed a lifetime had passed.

"You were right." He paused beside her at the veranda's edge and stared out at the lights of far-off businesses and homes that glowed like ghosts on the skyline. "What you said was right. I didn't tell you I was related to Hunter because I didn't trust what was between us."

He shifted, studied her profile, both angular and soft. "Growing up, I watched my mother waste her life by loving a man who didn't want her. I saw only the bad side of love, the one that causes pain, not joy. There was never any joy.

"Because of that, I made up my mind I would never let myself get anywhere close to feeling love. I didn't want to care about you, Melanie."

"That makes two of us," she said softly. She didn't look at him, just continued to stare out into the night.

"When I realized I was in love with you, the most important thing to me was not to lose you. And I thought I would if you knew I was related to the man who owns the horse that has brought your family to its knees." He raised a hand palm up, then let it drop back to his side. "I guess it sounds pretty convenient that I'd made up my mind to tell you about Hunter. But it's the truth."

She shifted to face him, her arms wrapped around her waist. "Why chance that if you thought you were going to lose me?"

"Because it was between us and I didn't want that anymore."

He paused to gather his thoughts. "When my mother begged me to never reveal the name of my father, she didn't do that out of any sense of love. By then, she hated him. Despised him for ruining her life. I realized if I continued to keep the promise I made to her, that all I would be doing was letting her bitterness cheat me out of the life that I thought, *hoped,* you and I could have together."

Because he couldn't help himself, he reached out, settled his hands on her shoulders. "I'm prepared to beg, if that's what it takes. You're the most important person in my life, Melanie. You *are* my life. I'm sorry I hurt you. Very sorry that I didn't trust you. I want another chance with you. I'm asking you to take another chance on me."

When he saw the tears swimming in her eyes, his heart constricted.

"Don't cry." It seemed he would beg after all. "Melanie, please, don't. Don't tell me I'm too late." Awkwardly he brushed at her tears with his thumbs. "Don't tell me I ruined everything."

"I thought you had," she said brokenly. "You hurt me, and I didn't want to hurt ever again." She closed her fingers around his wrists, watched the emotion leap into his eyes. "That's before I saw you almost die today. For me. You were ready to die for me."

"I could say the same thing about you. When you jumped on Alanssi's back, I thought he'd kill you. I thought I'd lose you forever. I don't think I'll ever get that image of you on his back, beating at him with your riding crop out of my head."

"I didn't plan to jump. I just…"

"Just what?"

"I knew if I didn't do something fast, he would kill you. Right then, I didn't care that you'd kept a secret from me. It didn't matter that you're related to the man who owns Apollo's Ice. All that mattered was that I might lose the person most important to me." She pressed a palm against his heart. "The man I love."

"Melanie." He kept his hands on her face, kissed her gently. "I want to spend my life watching you race our Thoroughbreds. Having you poke and prod at my bruised ribs. Helping you force enormous Christmas trees into impossibly tiny spaces."

"Painting all of the stalls in the stables Day-Glo yellow?" she murmured against his lips.

He inched his head back, narrowed his eyes as he gazed down at her. "Is that negotiable?"

"Absolutely not."

"I'll buy the paint."

He brushed a light kiss against her throat and made her sigh. "Smart move."

"Does this mean you'll give me another chance? *Us* another chance?"

"If I don't, I know I'll regret it for the rest of my life. I don't want to regret you, Marcus." She eased out a breath. "I think what's between us is a lot like racing."

"How so?"

"It's all about taking a gamble. That's what I'm going to do."

The weight on Marcus's chest released in a flood, pouring out of him as he slid his arms around her waist.

"Melanie Preston, you're the only woman who makes my heart race. The only woman who ever will. Forever."

She smiled her way into a long, slow kiss. "Forever," she murmured.

* * * * *

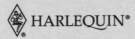

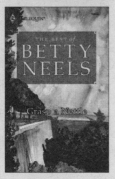